# Dongeng

ANNA TAN

Published by Teaspoon Publishing
http://www.teaspoonpublishing.com.my

ISBN: 978-967-15096-0-9

Writers in the Attic—

To 8k days
And being potatoes

# PRELUDE

He hesitates at the edge of the realm. Before him, the rainforest stands tall and mighty, enveloped in soft, cooling mists. There is the whisper of the wind in the leaves, the rumble of a waterfall in the distance, the rustling of creatures in the undergrowth, the caw of birds winging their way through the air. Overlaying it now is his deep sigh as he looks up into the sky with tears in his eyes.

"Go, before he finds you," Sang Kancil whispers.

"Thank you, my friend. And goodbye." He turns his back on the realm—on his childhood, on his family, on his friends, on the very core of his being—and steps into the world of man where his wife and newborn son await him. He hopes he has not been gone for too long. There is a sense of loss as the portal seals behind him with finality.

Behind him is a shriek he does not hear, a cry of rage raised because he is now unreachable, untouchable: *Pengkhianat! Traitor!* It reverberates in damp, dark caverns, burrows deep in rich fertile soil, screams in wide open skies. Inhabitants, both magical and non-magical, stop to listen, then go back to their busy lives.

Nothing is the same again on both sides of the door.

# CHAPTER 1

Sara opened her eyes slowly. She could smell the forest, which confused her. Hadn't she been on her way home? In the middle of the concrete jungle of Kuala Lumpur, hours away from anything green? Yet besides the smell of fresh greenery and moisture, she could also hear something like… running water? A tap? A river?  She shivered. Above her was a canopy of leaves. She sat up abruptly with a gasp, eyes wild as she looked around her. What *was* she doing in a forest?

*"Dia sudah bangun!"* someone said in Malay. Her brain scrambled to translate: *She's awake.*

She turned, holding the tattered green blanket nearer to her body. The back of her mind was churning. *Why is there a blanket? How long have I been here? How long have I been out? How did I get here?* Her eyes fixed on a slender girl dressed in a dark green kebaya who smiled and raised a tentative hand to wave.

"What—who—*siapa* you?" Sara fumbled, her brain struggling to figure out what to say.

The girl giggled. *"Tunggu."* She turned and seemed to disappear into the forest.

Sara did as instructed. She waited. What else was there to do? She wrapped the blanket around her, staving off the cold. *Why is it so cold?* She surveyed her surroundings. She was in a small clearing surrounded by thick, towering trees. She'd been lying on something like a dais covered in grass and moss. At its base, five smooth stones lay scattered, as if someone had dropped them. If they weren't as big as her palm, she'd think that someone had been playing Batu Seremban. A quick check showed that her handbag had landed up with her and—surprise— was intact with nothing missing. Getting a new identity card would have been a hassle, to say the least, besides having to cancel her supplementary credit card. Not that she'd ever used the thing. She picked up a stone, hefting it in her hand.

Soon enough, the girl returned with five others. Sara's hand curled around the stone, stepping back as she wondered if she would have to use it as a weapon. The two eldest, a male and a female, stepped forward and bowed. Sara imitated their gesture, wondering what was going on.

"*Selamat datang, Penglipur Lara. Beta mengalu-alukan kehadiran anda di alam kami,*" the man said with a flourish of his hand. He was of moderate height, with light brown skin and a wide smile. His hair was thick, a uniform peppery grey. Seventy-ish, nearing eighty, Sara guessed, mentally comparing him to the last time she'd seen her late grandfather. Sara thought that he would have been very handsome when he was younger. As it was, the wrinkles and lines on his face added stature and majesty to his sharp features.

"Greetings, Storyteller. We are honoured to have you here in our realm," the woman beside him translated, copying his gesture. She too had fine features, looking rather like the grand M in the James Bond movies, the one that died—Sara couldn't remember the actress's real name—but with thinner, sharper lines. The pair looked at each other and smiled.

"Uh, thank—*terima kasih?*" Sara squeaked. For once in her life, she wished that she'd kept her Malay in practice. It wasn't as if she didn't understand it or couldn't speak it; just that very often the words wouldn't come to her as fluently as she wished.

"We understand, my dear. We will speak English with you. After all, what we need from you is from that language," the woman said, laying a hand on her shoulder.

"What—"

"Come. Let us show you around and then we will tell you what we need."

"O-kay…?" What else could she say? Her hand tightened around the strap of her handbag, and she reflexively put the stone into the bag as she followed them.


Sara wasn't sure if she should start asking questions, but as they hiked farther into the forest and higher up through steep paths, she didn't have the breath to. All her energy was used up in trying to breathe while struggling to keep up with the silent people who seemed to ghost along the winding trek. It had been a long time since she had taken such a strenuous hike. She tried to remember when that had been and concluded: never. Still, she pushed on. The older pair and the young girl led the way, the other three flanking her sides and back, as if to make sure that she didn't escape. Sara looked around to see if she *could* escape. She was sure she couldn't run fast enough. Finally, they came to a stop.

"First of all, I suppose we should introduce ourselves. We are the Hidden People. My husband here is the Raja… king, as you call it, and I am his Permaisuri. I suppose that makes me a queen?" She laughed, a sound so calm and controlled, Sara wondered if it were real.

"The Hidden People?"

The Queen dipped her head slightly. "Yes. That's what we call ourselves."

Sara ran through her extensive knowledge of mythology, murmuring to herself. "Hobbits? No. Fairies? No, not quite. Elves?" Elves did quite seem to fit. She cast a critical eye on them. They were very beautiful people, though they didn't have pointy ears—who even thought up pointy ears anyway—and looked quite… Pan-Asian. Nothing was making sense. *Am I hallucinating? Am I in a coma? Maybe this is all just a very strange dream.* She pinched herself. Nothing happened. How did it work anyway? A pinch in a dream was still a dream-pinch. She couldn't see how that might affect the real world.

There was a short conference between the pair.

"Your people call us the Orang Bunian."

Sara's lips formed a silent O. Her interest had always been in Western Mythology, not in Eastern ones. However, no one had ever perfected living in a bubble, so she *had* heard of the Orang Bunian, however tangentially, though she didn't really know much about them except that they sometimes stole children. That made her pause. "Why did you kidnap me? I'm not a child."

"We know you are not. But you are the exact type of person who can help us."

"Help you? Help you do what?"

The Raja smiled. It wasn't a pleasant one; Sara thought there was something slightly predatory about it. "Look around you, Penglipur Lara."

Sara followed the sweep of his hands, taking in the view. They were on top of a hill. In the far distance, she could see dark clouds gathering. The wind blew nice and cool—almost foreign—and Sara shivered a little, hoping that it wouldn't rain. Down in the valley she could make out something like a town, a little on the small side, but the details were blurred. The rest of the view consisted of the rainforest and swamp. The wind shifted and a thick, muggy smell blew into her face. That felt a little more like home. She rubbed her tired eyes.

"I can't quite make out anything down there," she said, squinting to try to find a good view.

The Permaisuri's smile looked rather sad. "Exactly." Then they were moving again, away from the edge of the cliff, and Sara followed suit as they took a seat on the ground in a circle.

The Permaisuri looked once again at her husband and cleared her throat. "Once, a long time ago, we were a strong realm. The people of the Malay Peninsula knew and respected us. We did not meet often, but when we did, they were significant events. But things have changed. We've been forgotten and we have faded into the past—faded so far that we ourselves cannot remember everything that we were meant to be. Which is why we need you, Penglipur Lara. We have heard your stories, we have seen the way your words, silent and hidden as they are, have recreated the people you pass by every day. And we, the Hidden People, need you, the Storyteller, to revive our stories again."

The six Bunians looked at her expectantly. Sara's gaze shifted from one face to another, confusion clouding her thoughts.

"What? No."

"You can try…"

Sara shook her head. "No. This is crazy. I'm dreaming. This is not real."

The Raja and Permaisuri rose to their feet silently. His face was hard, almost angry, hers unreadable.

"It is real. Believe me." The Permaisuri's lips closed in a thin, sharp line.

Sara shook her head again. "What?"

The pair took a step back. The young girl clambered to her feet and ran to them, taking the Permaisuri's hand. Then they took another step back and faded from sight.

"What—wait, you can't leave me here!" Sara turned to look at the remaining three Bunians.

Their faces were stony with disappointment. Sara couldn't help thinking that it was very beautiful disappointment all the same. They too exchanged glances and nodded to themselves.

*What does that mean?* Sara got to her feet, hurrying after them, scrambling for words. "*Tunggu!*"

Down the path they went, gliding gracefully and silently, with Sara panting behind them, crashing through the brush. Fear gripped her again. What would happen to her if she was left in this forest? Would the animals eat her? Then again in all the time she'd been here she hadn't even heard the call of a bird. Was this Malaysia? Or was she stranded somewhere else altogether? Belatedly, she remembered the royal couple's welcoming speech. *Realm*, she'd said, but he'd said the word *Alam*, something she would have translated into *World* instead. Had she really stepped into another world?

She soon forgot the thought as the three Bunians came to a stop in front of her and held out their hands.

"Where are we?" she asked.

They pointed down a dark path.

She stepped nearer, trying to see. "There? Why won't you speak to me?"

Still, they gestured. She took small steps towards it, looking back at them frequently. At the edge of the shadows, she bent forward to peer into the darkness.

"I can't see—"

They pushed her forward, the end of her sentence converting into a shriek. She fell for a long time, screaming all the way.

# CHAPTER 2

This time, Sara didn't open her eyes. Instead, she laid back and breathed in. No more forest smells. She tried to listen instead, wondering why her head felt so fuzzy. Fuzzy and heavy. Where had she been? She tried to remember. She'd gone for a movie with Xiu. They had dinner. She'd taken the train home. She didn't remember walking back to the apartment, though. Yet, she was lying on something soft, something comfortable that smelt like home. She turned on her side and nuzzled deeper into the pillows and thick comforter. She was at home in bed. How did she get here? She didn't remember walking home. She could feel the sun streaming in, warming her face, the back of her eyelids.

*Shoot.*

She sat up abruptly. *I am* so *late for work. Helmi will definitely fire me this time.* Her phone alarm was set to ring every morning at six, so she couldn't understand why it hadn't woken her. She reached for her handphone, which was peeking out of her open handbag. It was dead. Sara groaned as she rubbed her face with the palms of her hands. What had she taken last night? It was impossible to be hungover on root beer, right? It wasn't even real beer! Just a lot of carbonated water. Too much sugar. She plugged in her handphone to charge and went to the kitchen to grab a cup of water. The microwave display blinked 11:37. Too late to rush. Another half an hour wouldn't make any difference. Not now.

A leisurely bath later, she turned her phone on to find 87 missed calls and 382 messages between SMS, WhatsApp, Facebook Messenger and Line. Why *did* she have so many messaging apps anyway? She stared at it in confusion. Opening Helmi's WhatsApp conversation, she scrolled through angry messages to concerned messages until they said 'Today'. Right after 'Thurs, 8 Sept.'

*What?*

She exited the program and looked at the calendar on her phone. Nothing made sense. She dug into her jeans pocket and looked for the movie ticket stub. 4 September, Sunday. That looked about right. She looked at her phone calendar again. It stubbornly said that it was 9 September. Friday. She was still staring at her phone when it started ringing.

Helmi's voice was panicky. "Sara? Sara? Are you okay? I saw you finally read my messages."

She was slightly bemused. "Yeah, yeah I'm fine, Mi."

"Where are you?"

"At home."

There was a sharp intake of breath. "At *home*? Where *were* you, Sara Liew Bao Yi?"

She was definitely in trouble. "I… I don't know, Mi. I… I remember going home after the movie with Xiu Li, and then I woke up and my phone was dead and I was going to message you that I'd overslept but… but my phone keeps telling me it's Friday. I don't understand."

She could almost feel Helmi's fear and frustration over the phone through the strain in his voice. "Sara, you watched the movie with Xiu Li five days ago. You haven't been to work for the whole week."

"It… it's really the ninth?"

"Sara, I'm coming over. Something is wrong."

"Okay. Okay."

"Don't go anywhere."

"I won't."

The call ended and Sara slowly lowered the phone to her lap. She stared at the date, willing it to turn back to the fifth. She couldn't understand where the days had gone. Xiu Li's messages were equally as frantic. Sara decided she'd better answer them while waiting for Helmi to arrive. Xiu Li would know she was back anyway. Helmi would have told her before leaving the office.

*'Hey. I'm… back. Or sth.'*

*'God. Sara whr were u?!'*

*'I dunno Xiu. Last thing I rmb was taking LRT after the show.'*

*'Whr u now?'*

*'Home. Helmi coming ovr.'*

*'Good. Go to docs.'*

*'Rly? Pls.'*

*'U were missing 5 DAYS girl. U gotta check!'*

*'Check what?'*

*'I dunno. Anything. Just in case.'*

*'Of?'*

*'What if u were raped?'*

Sara had no reply to that. She felt fine, bodily at least. Her head was still heavy so she went to her fridge and rummaged about for a Panadol. There were none in her fridge. A quick scan of her shelves did not reveal any hidden paracetamol anywhere so she went back to her charging phone and called Helmi.

"What happened?" he asked the minute it connected.

"Nothing, Mi. Chill. I just wanted to ask if you could get me a Panadol or something."

"Why?"

"Because I'm having a headache?"

"Okay. I'll swing by the 7-11 on the way over. Should be there in about ten, fifteen minutes. You sit tight okay?"

"Okay." Sara rolled her eyes and ended the call.

With a sigh, she thought about what to reply Xiu Li. Finally, she typed, *'Feeling fine. No strange body sensations. Anyway. Will see what Helmi says.'*


Sara's conversation with Helmi felt like a repeat of her WhatsApp conversation with Xiu Li, except that it was in grammatical—if not quite complete—sentences. She wasn't sure about the spelling. He made her tell him everything she remembered over and over again, from when she left the cinema up until she walked out of the train station and then waking up in her own bed, which wasn't much. At least the Panadol was starting to work so her head wasn't pounding anymore.

"I tell you, Helmi, I don't remember anything."

"Fine. So nothing out of the ordinary happened except you sleeping like the dead for four days. Even when we pounded on the door like we would break it down." Helmi ran a hand across the back of his head, scratching at the nape of his neck.

"Why didn't you?"

"What? Didn't—"

"The more important thing, Mi, is do I still have a job?"

He stopped pacing and looked at her. "Yes, yes you do. As long as you agree to go for a medical check-up. I'll… I'll put you on medical leave today and take the rest off your annual leave. Say it was an emergency or something."

"Thanks."

He cleared his throat. "Well, let's head to lunch and I'll take you to the clinic."

Sara grabbed her handbag, reaching into it to check if her wallet was inside. Her hand curled around something cold and smooth. Her belly clenched as she drew out a shiny stone.

Helmi's voice broke her from her reverie. "Sa? What's wrong?"

She opened her hand, showing him the stone. "It was a dream…"

"What was a dream?"

"There were these beautiful people. Like, you know, like… Legolas? No, not really. Like the one in the Hobbit. King Thranduil or something. Dark haired. Not white. Very… Well, almost Malay. But very good-looking. And his wife—well, I think she was his wife. Something like… no, not like Arwen. I was thinking of M in my dream, but a very fairy-like or elvish M?"

"You're not making any sense, Sa."

Sara snorted. "Of course not. It was just a dream."

"But the rock?"

She looked down at the rock in her hand. An involuntary shiver ran through her. "That's the funny part. This rock was from my dream."

Helmi led her back to the couch. They sat down turned in towards each other, knees touching. She was still holding the rock. He laid a hand on her knee.

"Tell me about this dream. Everything you remember about it."

Sara bit her lower lip. "I'll try. It's all a little fuzzy."

"I'll guide you. What happened at the start?"

"The start is really weird. I don't know… I woke up. But then I was holding this rock, and these people came and said hello. Or something."

"What people?"

"There was a girl first, and then the two I told you about. I think they said they were royalty. I'd picked up the rock then because—I'm not sure. I think I was afraid that some animals would attack me?"

"Where was this?"

Sara shrugged. "A forest of some kind."

"What were you doing in a forest?"

"I don't know, Mi. I told you it was a dream! It doesn't make sense." She could feel her voice rising in tone and in volume, her frustration spilling out to him. "Sorry. I'm sorry."

He raised his hands, palms outwards, placating. "No, no, that's fine. So, there's a king and a queen? Did they say of what?"

"Funny. I think I remember asking them that. Hiding people? Hidden people? Something like that."

Helmi hissed behind his teeth.

Sara looked at him curiously. "What?"

"Nothing. What happened next?"

"I think we went somewhere."

"Where?"

She shook her head slowly. "I don't know. We walked really far in the forest. I just remember that they were asking me for help. Me! Isn't that ridiculous?"

"What did they want you do to?"

"You're not taking this seriously, are you, Mi? It's just some weird dream I had when I was in coma or something."

Helmi nodded. "Let's get you to a doctor."

They were nearly at the clinic when another thought crossed Sara's mind.

"Mi, would you know anything about the Orang Bunian? They're like a Malay myth, aren't they?"

"Yeah. Why?" He glanced sharply at her. Sara was looking out the window, watching the cars pass by.

"Dunno. The name just came to mind. I think I heard about them recently."

"From who?"

"No idea."

"From your dream?"

Sara turned to look at Helmi. His hands were gripping the steering wheel tightly and there was a strange look on his face.

"What's wrong, Mi?"

"You said it before, Sa. The Hidden People. *Orang Bunian.*"

Sara swallowed nervously. "That's what I was dreaming about?"

Helmi pulled into a parking lot. Sara sighed and shook her head as she followed him into the clinic. He was quiet all through the doctor's visit.

After the doctor had given her a clean bill of health and they were back in the car, Sara turned to him quizzically.

"Mi? You didn't answer me."

"I'm not so sure it's a dream, Sara. The whole Orang Bunian thing worries me."

"Why? It's just a myth."

He started the car. "To you."

"What's that supposed to mean?"

"Sara, you're Chinese—"

"Malaysian."

"Yeah, whatever. But you're traditionally—ethnically? Or whatever—Chinese. You don't believe in these things. I do."

She turned to him, surprised. "You do? You didn't strike me as the superstitious type." She paused. "Aren't you Muslim, though? How does this fit with like your religious beliefs and stuff?"

"Well, culturally… I mean, my grandfather used to tell me these stories. It's—it's complicated."

"O-kay."

"But… well, would it be alright with you if I consulted a bomoh about it?"

"A bomoh? Really? How would that help?"

"Well, he can speak to the spirits. Um, and maybe he can speak to the Orang Bunian. To see if this was real."

"What do you mean by real? It's just a dream."

Helmi scratched at the back of his head again, driving one-handed. "Because it fits, kan? In the legends, those who wander into the Orang Bunian's sacred lands—or they were kidnapped, depending on the story—when they come back again, many years have passed."

Sara tried to wrap her head around it. "So time moves differently there?"

"Something like that. One day there is a few weeks here or something. I don't know. So maybe one night there for you became four days here. Makes sense?"

"Like Narnia."

Helmi shrugged.

"And you think talking to the bomoh will help?"

"Well, he might be able to tell us something. Or at least confirm that it's only a dream. Won't hurt, kan?"

Sara sighed and rolled her eyes. "I guess not."

Helmi pulled up at the guard house of Sara's apartment. "I'll ask around and find one with the right skills."

"Skills?"

"To see the spirits. Different bomohs have different skills. Not all of them can see spirits, or not all of them can communicate with the Orang Bunian. I think."

"So we need one who can talk to them?"

Helmi nodded. "Yea. Anyway, you're on medical leave until Monday. I'll see you on Tuesday."

"Thanks, Helmi."

"Just doing my job."

She smiled at him and thanked him again as she got out of the car. Closing the car door firmly, she waved as he drove off, watching until he was out of sight. At the back of her mind, an uneasiness started to prickle. *You're definitely doing more than just your job.*

She wasn't quite sure what she felt about that.

# EXPOSITION

The girl is safe. The girl is *nothing*. The girl doesn't see her. Isn't supposed to.

The Lang Suir rakes her long nails through her ankle-length hair, trying to smooth it down. She isn't jealous of the girl. The girl isn't pregnant. But she is important. Exactly *why* the Lang Suir doesn't know, but she knows the girl *has* to be important. The enemy wouldn't be interested in her otherwise. She trails the boy home instead. He enters a nondescript house with a once-familiar presence. She frowns, taking on her owl form. Dark is gathering and it's not unusual to see an owl this far out of the city. It's not common either, so she keeps out of sight, waiting for the boy to leave.

The boy hurries away. She creeps nearer to the house.

"What do you want?"

She startles at the voice.

"I can see you and I know what you are. There are no children here for you so why are you here?"

"You're *him*."

A frown crosses his face. "Who?"

"The enemy of my enemy is my friend," she says mockingly. "Will you be my friend?"

"No. It doesn't work that way. Why are you here?"

"They are watching her. Their forces are gathering. Would you know why?"

The frown intensifies. "Her? Who?"

"The girl! The girl the boy was with. The girl with the words of power and lack of defences."

"Sara?"

The Lang Suir smiles. She now has a name.

# CHAPTER 3

Helmi looped around the little roundabout heading to Sara's apartment a second time, trying to calm his nerves. He wasn't sure what it was—was he only worried because of the Orang Bunian? Or was there something else? Asking her to meet the bomoh had been a little harder than he'd expected. Sure, she had seemed somewhat receptive on Friday after the clinic, but there had been a bit of an odd vibe between them when he brought it up earlier today at work. He was quite sure it had nothing to do with the way Xiu Li was grinning at them from a few tables away.

"So, my grandfather knows this bomoh," he remembered saying, shifting his feet nervously until she looked up at him again and prompted, "And?"

"Would you be free tonight? He said that we could meet at eight-thirty most evenings. I thought… we might as well just get it over with."

She turned to stare at the clock. "Well, I don't drive and I don't really want to head home late, if you know what I mean."

"I know. I'll come pick you up."

"Oh." She thought about it and then nodded. "What time?"

"He stays about ten minutes from your place so I'll come over around eight? Eight-ten?"

"I guess that would be fine."

The clock on his dashboard showed that it was nearly ten past eight, so he took a deep breath and turned onto the road leading to her apartment. He waved at the guard, who let him in with a smile; Helmi figured he must have come often enough to be recognised by now. Sara was waiting at the bottom of her apartment block.

"You ready?" he asked as she got in the car.

"As ready as I can be."

Helmi checked his GPS. The short ride was silent, Helmi full of his own thoughts and misgivings, Sara biting nervously on her lower lip. They took another five minutes to find a place to park along the roadside.

The terrace house was dark as they approached. Helmi wondered if he'd gotten the right place, but the porch lights turned on just as the two of them reached the gate. The door swung open and an old man looked out at them with filmy eyes.

"Pakcik Rozaimi? I'm Helmi, Abdul Mansoor's grandson. I called you earlier today…" Helmi introduced himself, speaking in Malay.

The old man nodded. "Come in," he replied in the same language, waving them in.

Helmi let Sara enter first, turning to latch the gate before following them into the living room. He wasn't quite sure what he expected to find, but it definitely wasn't this. It looked like any other house: an old rattan couch with faded cushion covers, a low coffee table with newspapers scattered across it, an old CRT TV that flickered until the equally old man switched it off, a framed quote from the Quran above the TV, the fan spinning furiously above them all. Where were the occultic decorations? Crystal balls? Candles? Collection of herbs and coconuts?

He took a seat on the couch beside Sara, keeping a careful distance between them. He wasn't very orthodox in any way, but he didn't want to give Rozaimi the wrong impression. Rozaimi pulled up his seat opposite them whilst his wife laid a tray of drinks on the table. He seemed a little distracted, mumbling to himself on and off. Helmi watched him with sceptical eyes.

"I have never met anyone who has come back from the world of the Orang Bunian in such a short time," Rozaimi said suddenly, startling them. "Tell me about this dream."

Sara glanced at Helmi before beginning, initially stumbling over her words. Rozaimi listened intently, his dark eyes piercing hers, losing their filmy look.

"And you're sure it's a dream?" Rozaimi asked when she finished.

Sara twisted her fingers in front of her. "I don't know… but what else can it be?"

"Can you talk to them? The Orang Bunian? Would they tell you if it was real?" Helmi asked.

The bomoh's gaze shifted to him. "I have been talking to them, young Helmi. They spoke to me of your coming. They spoke to me of her. What I want to know is if your… friend here can recognise the difference between a dream and reality."

There was a short pause before she answered. "The thing is—I really can't recall exactly what happened. It feels as if everything was a blur. But if it's not a dream, then what is it?"

Helmi could hear the worry in Sara's voice. He reached out and grasped her hand, rubbing his thumb over it in what he hoped was a comforting way.

"You are quite remarkable, Penglipur Lara. The Raja of the Orang Bunian had hoped to wipe your mind of the experience after you rejected his call for help, but it appears that he was not quite successful."

"They *what*?" Helmi shot to his feet, hands clenched.

Rozaimi cleared his throat, looking at Sara. "It was non-invasive. All they did was cover her with a glamour."

"A glamour? Why?"

Sara reached up and grabbed his hand, pulling him down to his seat. "Can you explain to me what they wanted? I cannot remember what it was clearly. I would like to know."

Rozaimi studied her face for a while before answering. "They believe that you have powers, Penglipur Lara. They think that their world is in danger and only you can help them."

"Why me? I don't even really know who they are. Why not someone like Helmi who has grown up knowing about them and their legends?"

"Because of who you are, Penglipur Lara. Because when you have learnt their stories you can retell them to the world." The old man looked eagerly at Sara, his eyes now as piercing as an eagle's.

Sara laughed. "Tell it to who? I'm just a clerk, Pakcik. I file papers. That's it. Any stories I tell is just to myself. No one listens to me."

"But you can. You have the power and the capability," he insisted.

She shook her head. "Helmi will tell you that all this storytelling has only gotten me in trouble. Right, Mi?"

Helmi felt caught. "Well Sa," he started cautiously, "I suppose it depends on how you end up using it? I can't deny you do have a way with words."

She turned sharply away from him, looking at Rozaimi instead. Helmi wasn't sure if she was blushing or crying.

"So all they want me to do is tell their stories?"

Rozaimi shook his head. "Yes, they want you to do that. But they also want you to go live with them for a while so that you can also tell them about themselves. Because the magic is dying and they are forgetting. And soon, they will be no more."

"No." Helmi was surprised to find that he was speaking, that he had risen to his feet again, standing between Sara and Rozaimi like a shield.

"Mi?"

"No, Sara. You can't do that. That one 'short period' they took you ended up being four, almost five days. You go in again and… what if you never come out?"

"Helmi, this is not your decision to make," Rozaimi said, looking anxiously at Sara. "You can't decide for her."

"Sa, please," Helmi pleaded, kneeling before her. Shock was written all over her face, but he couldn't spare the time to think about it. "If you won't think of me, then think of Xiu. Think of your family. You'll be gone—and dead to us—maybe forever."

"I—Well, I don't know, Mi. It doesn't even make sense. Can I think about it, Pakcik? Does the answer need to be now?"

The old man nodded slowly. "You can think about it, Penglipur Lara. But do not take too long. They do not have long. Well, none of us do."

Helmi and Sara took their leave, thanking Rozaimi for his help. They walked out slowly to the car, Helmi glancing nervously at Sara often. She walked, her head bent, studying the path before her.

"What did you—" she started saying just as Helmi said, "So how do—"

Helmi gestured for Sara to go ahead.

"What did you mean in there?" Sara said.

"About what?"

"Being dead to you all forever?"

"It's part of the myth, Sara. Those who decide to live with the Bunian—when, *if,* they emerge in the world again, many years would have passed in our world. We may all be dead by the time you come out again."

"Not Narnia. It's Rip Van Winkle," Sara murmured to herself.

"What?"

"An English myth."

"Oh."

They fell silent, standing by Helmi's car. Finally, he looked up at her again. "So how do you feel about this? Is this something you think you would be able to do?"

"You want me to do it?"

"No, well, yes, maybe. If it's something that you want to do. But don't stay with them. I mean, you can write about them from here. That should be perfectly fine, I think."

"Maybe if we had a way to…" She shook her head. "Never mind. Let's go home, Mi. I can't think about this anymore tonight."

# DEVELOPMENT

He paces. That's all he can manage to do ever since the Lang Suir left. He's been pacing for weeks now, finally getting all the exercise his children and grandchildren have been urging him to get. It doesn't help the worry, just makes him even more antsy.

He wants to go back. He wants to confront *him*, ask what *he's* up to now. What twisted story has *he* been telling his people? What lie has *he* created this time? But he can't. The portal is closed. The door has been shut to him for fifty years now. *Fifty years.* His heart stutters and he sits down with a bump. No, not now. He can't die now. He must go back. He must find out. He must *know*. But how? They won't talk to him, not since…

*The enemy of my enemy is my friend. The enemy…*

He slumps against the wall. He doesn't know if he should take her up on the offer or if he even still can, weeks after the fact. He doesn't know how to contact her. Or if he should. He wants to go *home* now but he can't.

All he can do is pick up the phone to call his son and ask if he can visit. It won't help, but at least he'll be close. Close enough to ask. Close enough to pry. His daughter-in-law's cooking is only a secondary temptation. He pretends it's his main goal.

# CHAPTER 4

Nothing out of the ordinary happened over the next three weeks and the memory of the incident started to fade in Sara's mind. Still, she made an effort to not stay out late, just in case of a repeated incident (she had wanted to call it a kidnapping, but that didn't seem quite right) and also just in case it had been something else altogether, and not the Bunians. Xiu Li didn't bring up the incident and neither did Helmi, though he often looked out of his office at her as if to check if she was still there. It felt a little weird.

So when Sara woke up early one Sunday to find a bird perching at the foot of her bed, she was shocked. She stared mutely at the animal, wondering how it had gotten in. It wasn't any bird she remembered seeing before; pigeons and crows were what she was used to, not great big birds in bright golden plumage with a flaming horn.

"Hai, Penglipur Lara," the bird said.

"What the—" She bolted upright. Rubbed her eyes. Stared.

"Yes, I'm here."

"Who—what—"

The bird chuckled. Sara slapped her face lightly, wondering if she was awake.

"You're awake, Sara," the bird said. "Let me introduce myself. My name is Garuda. Ah, I see a spark of recognition there. You have heard of me, yes?"

Sara nodded mutely. *Why is this happening?* She tried to pinch herself.

"I am a legend. Everyone knows of me. Which is why I have been chosen to come and speak to you. Again."

Sara pulled the blankets up around her body, as if building a wall between the mystical bird and herself. "Again?"

"Well, the Orang Bunian tried—and failed. Thus, again."

Realisation dawned upon her. "Oh!"

"Right now, I deem that you are not sufficiently awake. If you could wash up and maybe make a cup of your preferred caffeine fix, that would be great." He started to fly off, then settled down again, staring at her with piercing eyes. "I assure you I am not a dream."

Garuda flew out of the room without a backward glance leaving Sara staring at the open door. In a daze, she stumbled out of bed and into the shower, where she took an extra-long, extra-hot shower. She left feeling refreshed and comfortable, having quite forgotten about Garuda. She was boiling water to make instant noodles and tea when Garuda re-materalised and perched on one of the dining chairs. Surprised, she threw the hot water at him, screaming.

"What was that for?" Garuda said in annoyance as he flapped frantically out of the way.

She stared at him. "You're not a dream!"

"I told you that already," he huffed, settling on a dry chair.

"Okay. Yes. You did. I forgot. Sorry." She hurried to wipe up the spilt water and then stopped to stare at the bird.

"Go on, you were in the middle of making breakfast."

Sara opened the packet of Maggi Kari, noting distractedly that her hands were shaking as she poured the flavouring powder into the bowl. She managed to pour hot water into the bowl and into her tea cup without spilling anything. When she was finally settled at the table with food and drink, she took a deep breath, grateful that she hadn't dropped anything.

She looked expectantly at Garuda. "So…"

"Go ahead," the bird said politely, cocking his head to one side. "I'll talk while you eat."

He waited until Sara had started eating before he cleared his throat. "You read fairy tales, don't you?"

Sara looked up at him and nodded.

"And you know Tinkerbell's story."

"The Barrie version or the Disney version?"

A smile crossed his face. "Ah, most people would not even think to ask that. The Disney version."

"Well, yes."

"At that tragic moment when Tinkerbell is dying and Peter is trying to save her, what does he do? He asks all the boys and girls in the world to clap for her. The more that clap, the more that acknowledge her existence, the faster she recovers. It's the same thing. Your belief and your stories fuel our continued existence."

Sara swallowed. "The NeverEnding Story."

"Ah yes, yes, something like that."

"So, you are being forgotten and you want me to be like him and save your world?"

Garuda's grin looked almost mischievous. "Yes and no. You see, we're in this unique position of being part of stories told in a language that is confined to these borders. And as much as we can try to keep ourselves alive in the Kisah Dongeng, hikayat and folklore of these people, we won't get very far. Once our language dies out, we will die too."

"Your language? Dying out? Malay is the official language of Malaysia. It's not going to die out. Not like all the other little dialects and tongues used here. I mean, if you were saying that Iban legends or Dayak legends were dying out, I'd believe you. But Malay? I mean, everyone in this country of 30 million people knows the language." It was true. She spent eleven years in school learning the language. She may not be fluent… but at least she knew it.

"Knowing the language and understanding the language and culture are two totally different things," Garuda said stiffly.

"Fine. Then why choose me? Choose someone who speaks the language fluently, why don't you? By our politician's definitions I'm just an immigrant anyway. Did you just randomly point at any old passer-by or something?"

Garuda was silent for a while. "Sara, believe me when I say this. We chose you for very specific reasons. First of all, for your love of fairy tales and all things magical. The way you embrace not only the White fairy tales you grew up with, but the way you're interested in Eastern fairy tales and magical, mystical creatures. You may not know much about us yet but we hope that you will accept our invitation to come find out about our world. You'll find that we are just as wonderful, just as colourful, and, hopefully, just as worthy as those in far away, cold countries.

"Secondly, you have the capacity to understand and love us. We could have gone to any Malay speaker who grew up with us in their culture, but they do not appreciate us anymore. We are part of the 'old' to be discarded for prosperity and development and progressiveness. You love all things old and you integrate them with the new.

"Thirdly, and lastly, you are representative of the audience we are trying to reach. The English-speaking world. Our stories need to be told in languages other than ours to keep our heritage alive. As I have said before, if the appreciation of the Malay language—beautiful as it is—dies, so do our stories. But if you can write them in English—showcase them to the larger world—then maybe, just maybe, we will continue to live on in a new way. And maybe more people would be interested in learning our language too."

Garuda looked at her pleadingly. "Please come. Just for one day. I won't repeat the Orang Bunian's mistake. You won't disappear for four days and return not knowing what happened. I'll take you into our Realm and one day there really will be one day here."

Sara looked at him uncertainly. "Just one day. No surprises."

"No surprises," he promised. He seemed to think about something for a moment and then said, "I'll even help you get to the White Fairy Kingdom where you'll be able to meet some of those foreign fairy tale beings you like so much."

Sara bit her lip. It was a very tempting proposition. "When will this be? Now?"

"Whenever you're comfortable doing it. Today, tomorrow, next week. But as soon as possible, of course. Please?"

"Fine. Fine, I'll do it—" she held out a hand to stop Garuda's jubilation, "but not today. I'll have to make arrangements. Let Helmi know where and when I'm going—and I need you to be able to be contactable. In case he worries."

"Contactable?"

"Yes. Helmi must have a way to contact you. In case I disappear for more than a day. As planned."

Garuda nodded. "I'm sure we can arrange something." He stuck out a talon which Sara took. They shook on it.

"Next week."

Garuda cocked his head to the left.

"The best day would be Saturday. In case..." Sara let her sentence trail off. She shook her head. "Unless something changes, Saturday will be the day."

Garuda nodded. "I'll be back next week." The golden bird preened with happiness and flew out the window.


With Garuda gone, Sara tried to think through what he had said. It made sense, on one level, but it was a scary proposition. What was she getting into? Why was she letting herself be persuaded by magical creatures she knew nothing about? What if Garuda turned out to be a trickster? She tried to convince herself that he was not. But how would she know? Seeing that he was such a slick talker? Impossible. This was just impossible. But she had just said she would go, so she decided she would at least give him a chance. The benefit of a doubt.

She sighed, got up and went to wash her dishes. Then she washed her clothes. Next, she started cleaning the house. Finally, running out of things to do to put off the inevitable, she took her handphone, sat down and pondered what to message Helmi.

*'Hey, so something happened today. You free to talk?'*

Within seconds, he replied, *'I'll call you in a bit.'*

She sat back and waited, rehearsing her lines in her head. When he finally called, she blurted out everything in one breath, barely waiting for him to say anything other than hello. There was silence over the line.

"Hello? You still there?" she asked.

"Yeah, yeah I am. Okay. Uh, you know what. I'm coming over."

"You don't have to, Mi."

"This is easier to talk about face to face, Sara. Uh, tell you what. You get ready and I'll pick you up for dinner. Sound alright? It might take me one hour to get there."

"Forget it, Helmi. It's crazy for you to drive so far through all that traffic."

"It's no bother, Sa. See you then."

He ended the call before she could protest further. Sara wanted to scream in frustration. She'd just wanted to ask for a favour. A simple favour. He was getting rather overprotective and overbearing, in her opinion.

She leaned back on the couch, wondering what to wear.

It was nearing 8:30 p.m. by the time Helmi arrived, almost thirty minutes later than he'd projected. Helmi refused to let her bring up the subject until he'd driven to the nearest mamak stall, parked and they'd ordered their food. Then he'd taken a big breath, sighed, and asked, "Are you sure about this, Sara?"

"No, I'm not sure about this. But what am I to do?"

"Just say no. It's ridiculous. It's dangerous."

"Look, Helmi, I've been thinking about it. Do you want to live in a world where your folklore doesn't exist anymore? Where all the stories you've grown up with have disappeared?"

Helmi looked confused. "I don't really care, Sara."

"Well, I do. I love stories, Helmi, and I'm just now discovering yours—your heritage. Mine too. And I don't want to just discover them now only to have them disappear."

"But you don't have to go in there to… write whatever it is that you're supposed to write. Pakcik Rozaimi said that you could do it from here."

"*You* said that I could do it from here. He didn't give an opinion about it."

"You're twisting my words."

"No, I'm not. You're the one who's trying to twist things around."

They glared at each other in frustration.

"All I'm asking is for you to wait for me and contact Garuda if I'm not back within the day. Don't you get it? I'm taking precautions here. I'm laying out plans so that you know where to find me and who to press if I never make it back."

"You're making plans and precautions with a fictional character which won't help me very much in making a police report of your disappearance."

"Why would you—"

"Hi, I'd like to report a disappearance. My friend has been kidnapped by Garuda and the Orang Bunian. Do you know how crazy that sounds?" His voice started to rise.

Sara looked around, hoping that no one was eavesdropping on them. "Sshhh, not so loud. Look, I'm not asking you to make a police report."

"No," he interrupted her. "You're asking me to trust a legend that I haven't seen in my life and not question if you're still sane."

Sara's fingers curled around the edge of the table, her fingers white with the pressure. "You think I'm crazy? That's it? What happened to your worry about real hauntings and involving your local bomoh to see if the spirits are really talking to me? You believed him, didn't you? Why don't you believe me?"

Helmi looked down at his food miserably. "It's… oh never mind."

They ate in silence, mutually ignoring each other. Behind them, a football game started playing on the big screen and the roadside stall soon started filling up with people.

"Look, Sa, I'm sorry. Go ahead and do what you need to. I—I'll… if anything happens, I'll come after you."

"Thanks, Helmi. Don't worry. Nothing will happen."

# CHAPTER 5

Saturday dawned dark and gloomy. Just past 7:00 a.m., Sara paced the room, waiting for Helmi to arrive. She heard shuffling outside and swung the door open just as he was raising his hand to knock.

"So, we're all ready?" a bright voice said out of nowhere, making both of them jump. She turned to see that Garuda had materialised on the couch.

"You're Garuda," Helmi said flatly as he slipped off his shoes and walked into the living room.

"At your service, young Helmi bin Rashid."

"How did—"

"I know everything about you, young man."

Helmi turned to Sara. "You told him about me?"

Sara looked perplexed. "No. I just mentioned that you'd be here to make sure I'm okay."

"I do know how to do research, you know. Even if I am a mystical being."

"You googled me."

The bird coughed nervously. "I read your diary."

"How the hell did you—"

"You forget, I am mystical. And you are away at work all day. Don't worry. I will keep your secrets. For now."

Helmi clenched his teeth. "Thank you, I suppose."

"Anyway, he is here, so we should be on our way." Garuda nodded at Sara. She stepped towards him and was about to take his wing when Helmi stopped them.

"Wait. How do I contact you?"

Garuda looked at him scathingly. "Fine." He ruffled his wings, turned his head and pulled out a loose feather from his plumage. Helmi reached out to take the glinting feather from Garuda's beak.

"Keep it safe, young man. And don't call me for no reason."

"What do I do with this?"

Garuda clicked his beak. "If you need me, burn it. I will come to you."

Helmi nodded.

"Now if we can leave…?"

He grasped her hand, squeezing it once. "Sara… stay safe."

Sara watched Helmi's face as the room—and him—faded away. She wasn't sure why he looked so depressed.

"You like him, do you not?" Garuda said, interrupting her thoughts.

"What?"

"You think he would make a good mate."

Sara laughed. "He would, but it would never work."

"Why not? Are you two not compatible? He seems to care very much for you too."

Sara shrugged, more interested in watching how her apartment had faded and how a verdant rainforest was coming into view.

"Do you not think so?" Garuda pressed.

"He's very nice, Garuda," Sara replied. "But our outlook on life is far too different. As are our faiths."

"Faith?"

"Religion. Beliefs. The thing that makes wars."

"Ah, that. But people have resolved that."

She smiled wryly. "Maybe, but not in our country. Not in a good way, at least. Let's not talk about that. Tell me where I am."

Garuda glanced piercingly at her, but did not press the issue. He cleared his throat. "You are now in Alam Dongeng."

"Alam Dongeng," she repeated under her breath. "World… Realm? Of fairy tales?"

"Yes, this is where all our Kisah Dongeng have been birthed and nurtured and cherished. Shall we?"

"Shall we what?"

"Take a walk through this world, of course. If you would let go…"

"Oh. Oh yes, of course." She released her grip on Garuda's wing, realising for the first time how tightly she'd been clinging on to it.

Garuda flexed his wings and took to the air. He hovered at eye-level somewhat ahead of her to the right. "Our realm has many beautiful creatures, some similar to the Western fairy tale creatures you are used to. Of course, we do have our differences. Some are larger differences, some are merely cosmetic. And some, of course, are starting to be taken over by the larger, louder narratives of the West."

He turned to face Sara, as if wanting to see if she was following. She nodded.

"We also have many… frightening creatures, creatures which have not yet been sanitised and cleaned up for children's consumption. The youths of today love the vampires of the west because their danger has been romanticised. But none will look on the Pontianak without fear. Yet they are in most respects almost the same. They emerge at night and they drink blood. One is loved, one is hated. Why?"

Sara glanced around nervously.

"But children like fear, do they not? They like horror stories and things that make them shiver."

"Well, not me," Sara replied.

"Once, fear was necessary."

They'd been walking for some time in the rainforest, the only sounds surrounding them the cawing and tweeting of various birds, the rustle of the undergrowth as unseen animals passed by and the crunching of Sara's feet on the path. They stopped at a place that seemed vaguely familiar to Sara.

"Have I been here before? When—" she stopped, unable to articulate the words; the fear was so strong in her.

"Yes. This is the Orang Bunian's stronghold. You will see them soon, unless you wish…?"

"No, I'll face them," Sara said resolutely, even if her face felt pale and drawn.

"They'll be bringing others of their kind."

"Their kind—?"

Garuda seemed to think about it for a while before answering her. "The other Orang Halus—fairy folk—of this realm. Did you think they were the only ones?" The bird cocked his head to one side, as if challenging her.

"No—I mean, I don't know."

"Well, you'll see them. They're coming now. The Orang Bunian you have met. The Hidden People, they call themselves."

Sara recognised the Raja and Permaisuri of the Bunians as they passed, exchanging cold nods.

"These are the Orang Ketot—dwarves, I think you might compare them to?" Garuda started to name each of the beings that were congregating in the wide clearing. "Orang Kenit—magical beings."

The ground began to shake and Sara grabbed on to a tree to steady herself, glancing around wildly. A dark shadow fell upon them and four large feet appeared at the edge of the clearing.

"Ah, those would be the Gergasi."

"There really are giants!" she said in astonishment.

More rumblings followed and a smaller giant passed by. Sara glanced up at them.

"That is the Gedembai."

"A different kind of giant?"

Garuda seemed to find some difficulty in explaining. "Well, she, uh, she can turn things to stone."

"Like Medusa."

Garuda made a gesture, something like a shrug. "No idea what that is." He turned to the Raja Bunian and said, "Shall we start then?"

"We wait, Tuan, for one more," the Raja replied. "The Bidadari will come for they need to relate our words to the Duyong who cannot survive here."

Sara murmured to herself, "Duyong." She knew what those were. They were mermaids. But Bidadari? Weren't those angels?

But Raja Bunian was calling them to court now. Sara couldn't help comparing him to the Fairy Queen, before wondering why there wasn't a Fairy King. Had there ever *been* a fairy king? The Lore hadn't been very clear on that—there might have been something in Shakespeare—but definitely Titania got more publicity than any of her supposed husbands.

The Raja spoke in a measured, mellifluous voice, much like the first time she'd met him, and now, in the presence of so many other beings, Sara wondered why she had been so afraid of him then. Being kidnapped had possibly been a major factor, but his charm was also evident.

Garuda nudged her.

"What?"

"You're falling for his spell."

She shook her head to clear her mind. He was talking again about the need to save their land from dying, from fading, and she could see that all the other creatures were nodding in agreement. What would happen if she said no, she wondered. Would they all turn against her? And now they were all turning to her, looking expectantly.

"Go on, say your piece," Garuda urged.

"What if I don't know what to say?"

"Trust your heart."

Sara personally hated that phrase. What did one mean 'trust your heart'? She didn't trust her heart. Her heart was perfectly capable of wanting two conflicting things at the same time. It was perfectly alright with loving and hating the same thing as well. This was not a time to trust her heart. This was a time to… she wasn't very sure. But they were waiting for her response, so she had to think of something to say.

She rose to her feet. "Uh, hi. Well, to be honest… what you ask of me is very difficult. I have to admit that… well, there is no other way to put it. I am an Anglophile. I love all things British, the West has a hold of my heart. But… but I think I feel you too. What you are, who you aspire to be, the dangers… I can't say it hasn't happened in the West. Their stories have been subverted and changed and remoulded and… well, if you don't take hold of your own narrative, then that's what's going to happen to you and yours too. Which is why I say I'm not the best advocate for you. I don't know enough about you, or what you stand for. I don't know anything of where you come from or why you came to be.

"What will happen if I change your stories? What will happen if… if I misrepresent you? It's too difficult. I don't want to bear that burden. I grew up on Enid Blyton and Tolkien and CS Lewis. I didn't grow up with your Penglipur Lara and your folktales and your myths. I do not believe that I can do you justice."

The crowd started to murmur amongst themselves. Sara shook her head, tears in her eyes.

"I thought about this very long and very hard. Helmi thinks I'm crazy. And you know what, I probably am. Maybe you should ask him to do this, Raja Bunian. He is the one who knows of you. Who knows without being told why I should fear you or why I should not. He wouldn't have been afraid of you as I was when you took me, because he would have known who you were. He wouldn't fall for your charms because he knows your wily ways."

"But maybe that is why we need you," a large bird said gently as it came to land beside Garuda. The blue bird nodded to its comrade. "Garuda."

"Jentayu," Garuda acknowledged in return.

Jentayu turned his gaze back to Sara. "Because we need something to help us keep up with the times before we die in obscurity."

"I… I can't. It's not my burden to bear."

"And so you would let us die." Garuda's voice was cold. Cutting.

"It would be appropriation for me to dare to take your voices," she said in a small voice. There it was at last, her last niggling doubt. She didn't want them to die.

Garuda scoffed. "We are not Americans to be worried about such things."

"But there are others who will be."

"Who *might* be. But would you rather we die altogether than to at least battle for survival?"

Sara didn't like the militaristic undertones. She didn't like this discomfort in her heart. She didn't like where this was going, as if it was going to be her fault that this world died, when she never had any stake in it at all.

Jentayu spoke then, feeling like a voice of reason. "You are a child of Malaysia too, Sara. Your stake in them is the stake of all Malaysians—ensuring that you have a legacy to carry on. That you will not all be white-washed and your voices silenced."

There was bitterness in her voice as Sara replied, "but I am white-washed."

"Then take this as your redemption."

# ACCELERANDO

The house is quiet. His son and daughter-in-law have gone out somewhere—he does not know where, does not ask. They are adults, after all, and he is merely a visitor—and the boy is most likely still asleep. He lingers at the dining table, still sipping at his cooling coffee when the front door opens and the boy walks in.

"Morning, 'tuk," the boy mumbles. He looks restless, antsy.

"Where did you go so early in the morning?"

The boy sighs and slides into a chair, leaning slumped over the table. "What if she doesn't come back?"

Fear grips his heart. "Why wouldn't she?" He's not sure if *she* refers to the girl his grandson has been seeing or if it's someone else—if it's that *someone* trying to seduce him. *The enemy of my enemy…*

"I don't trust him."

"Him?" He cannot read the boy's mind, but it's clear that he's jumping from thought to thought, sowing marbles in their houses, calculating with each click to see who will end up with the most seeds in his store. Who is he playing against and what's at stake? "You should never trust Putera Aria." He speaks from bitter experience. *Not Putera now—Raja.* He doesn't correct his mistake.

"Who?" But the boy doesn't wait for him to explain. "Garuda. Can I trust Garuda?" he asks, looking up with an expression that is all at once desperation and fear and worry and calculation.

He wonders what his grandson has become, even as he nods once. Garuda can be trusted. The kings of old—the kings of *men* of old—had trusted him. Garuda is honourable even in his pride and foolhardiness, is said to be honourable even to the point of death. If Garuda is on their side, at least he knows truth will be upheld. "Where is she?" he asks, although he already knows the answer.

"Alam Dongeng. This morning. I went to see her off."

Pain and sorrow pierces his heart. He doesn't speak of it, and the boy, caught up in his own misery, doesn't ask.

# CHAPTER 6

Mary Hays peered at the strange trees surrounding her. "I don't believe I have ever been to this part of the Fairy Kingdom before." It felt hot and muggy, unlike the cool breeze they'd been having earlier. It was also surprisingly bright, seeing that it was supposed to be a little past midnight.

Ataneq slowed, looking around as well. "It feels different," he said, before hurtling down the path.

"Slow down, Neq, I'm not as young as I used to be!" Truth was, Mary was feeling every bit of her seventy years as the heat folded around her. She took off her shawl and used a corner to wipe her sweat. "Oh my! Why is it so hot here?"

The adlet stopped. "I do believe that we've been joined by a new fairy kingdom," he said as he waited for her to catch up. "Isn't that exciting?"

"It is. But how does it happen?" Mary had been in and out of the Old Fairy Kingdom ever since she was eight—ever since that meddling old crone, Baba Yaga, had lured her sister in. Her grandmother, the Fairy Queen, was against their presence in the Kingdom, harbouring her anger and hatred against her supposedly human father, only to find that Darrick Hays was half-elf and half-human. Since then, they'd been given grudging permission to enter the Kingdom. Whilst the Dragon's decree had allowed their friends access as children, Jane and Mary had continued to enjoy continued access long past adulthood because of their blood ties.

"I don't know. I'm not entirely sure how I stumbled into this one either."

They walked down the overgrown path, Ataneq slowing his pace to match Mary's. He looked at her with worry sometimes. She'd been a bright, young girl when he'd first met her, and now she was old and grey while he hadn't changed a bit. The ravages of time. He hated it. He was glad now that he had declined Baba Yaga's offer to turn him back into a human. Too many years had passed—his wife and sons would have died by then—and there was nothing for him to return home to. This was now his home, for better or worse.

"Does it look to you like there's some sort of plague here?" Mary asked, dislodging him from his melancholic thoughts.

"Is there?" He peered closely at the tree he was standing next to. "Well, it looks like a tree. It's a little… pale? But maybe that's just what trees in this place look like. You know, maybe they're a light-bark type of tree."

"But I don't think they're supposed to be slightly transparent, do you? Do you think we should ask Euthalia for her opinion?"

"I don't see why not." On second thought, Mary was right. The tree didn't just look pale—it was a little translucent. Another thought struck him. "I suppose these trees can talk to the dryads?"

"How would I know? Can't all trees talk to dryads?"

"Well, how were you planning on calling Euthalia then?"

"Oh. I hadn't thought that far. I just assumed that we could call her and she'd appear as she always did."

"We can try."

Mary and Ataneq took turns calling for the dryad by name. When she didn't appear after a few minutes, Ataneq shrugged and said, "I suppose that answers it. These trees probably don't talk to the dryads. Or, not yet anyway, if they really are from a new kingdom."

Mary looked around. "So, should we go on or do we go back?"

"Oh, onwards, of course!" Ataneq grinned. "It has been a long time since we had a new adventure!"

"Every day is an adventure with you, adlet," she teased in reply. "I never know when you'll turn 'round and try to eat me!"

The half-man, half-dog laughed, wagging his tail. "You know I'll never eat you. I don't like the taste of stringy old women!"

Unlike the Old Fairy Kingdom, where there wasn't much in the way of local animals, Mary was surprised to find that the underbrush and the skies were filled with fauna she had never seen before. A small deer-like animal skipped out of the bushes almost in front of them, stared in bewilderment and ran off. The birds were busy calling to each other high above, in something that sounded like speech, although Mary couldn't understand any of the words.

"Don't turn now, Mary, but I do think that deer thing is following us," Ataneq whispered in her ear.

"Why? And how do you know?" she whispered back.

Ataneq sniffed and touched the side of his nose.

"Does it seem to you that the birds are talking about us?" Mary whispered after a while.

"Maybe. But I don't understand their language."

Mary had a vague feeling of disquiet, as if things—creatures—were following them. Try as they might, Mary could not see them and Ataneq did not smell anything other than the faint musk of the tiny deer.

A crashing in the brush ahead made them jump. Mary gripped Ataneq's arm tightly when a troop of monkeys emerged right in front of their path. Ataneq tried to push Mary behind him to protect her, but when he turned at her gasp, he saw that the little deer had appeared on the path behind them, blocking their exit. The deer ignored them, squeezing past to confront the monkeys. There was an exchange of foreign words before the deer turned to look at them, seeming to nod at a path to their left. It then turned back to continue debating with the monkeys in sharp, loud noises.

Ataneq hurried down the path, Mary following closely behind.

"Where does this go?" she asked breathlessly.

"I don't know!"

"Then why are we following it?"

"The deer thing wanted us to!"

"And you trust it?"

"It just saved us!"

Mary couldn't argue with that so she saved her energy for panting as they continued down the path. They came to a stop at the edge of a clearing filled with many different types of humanoid creatures. In the middle of the clearing appeared to be an Asian girl flanked by two large birds. She seemed rather distressed.

"Oh my," Mary said. She said it rather loudly, being out of breath and out of sorts. Everyone turned in their direction.

The birds flew over, looking at them curiously.

"Who are you?" the golden one asked.

"Oh! You speak English!" Mary exclaimed. "Could you tell me what that little deer-like creature was? And what it was saying? It seemed to want us to come here. Oh and the birds, talking over our heads, although what they were saying I really couldn't tell. And your poor trees—are they ill?"

The birds exchanged glances.

"Sang Kancil directed you here, you say?" the blue one asked. "Curious."

"But you have not answered our question yet. Who are you and where do you come from?" the golden one insisted.

Mary blushed and held out her hand. "Oh, where are my manners! Mary Hays, pleasure to meet you. I come from Great Britain. You are...?"

A ripple of murmurs spread through the watching crowd.

"Garuda, at your service," the golden bird bowed slightly. "And my companion Jentayu," the blue bird made a similar bow, "but how are you here? And who is your companion?"

"Oh, we came through the Old Fairy Kingdom, of course. Though we're not entirely sure where we are right now. This is my friend, Ataneq. He's an adlet."

"The Old Fairy Kingdom?" the girl blurted, her hands pressed to her cheeks. "It's connected here?" She turned to Garuda. "So you weren't lying! You *were* going to bring me there!"

"Where is here, dear?" Mary asked her gently.

"Malaysia. I mean, well—this is Alam Dongeng, they say."

"Malaysia." Mary twirled the word in her mouth. She wasn't sure if she'd heard of the place before, but after all, it had been a long time since she had studied geography or looked at a world map. "Alam...?"

"Why would I lie?" Garuda was saying to the girl, looking slightly uneasy about it.

"Will I see real fairies then? And elves? And dragons?" the girl continued, tugging at Mary's sleeve.

Ataneq cleared his throat. "Could someone please explain what's going on?"

From Garuda and the girl Sara's confused, conflicting and overlapping conversations, it appeared to Mary that Garuda and the elf-like people had colluded to lie to Sara and bring her over to their version of a Fairy Kingdom. The bird had promised—lied, rather—that if she would follow him there, he would take her to see the fairy tales she'd cherished in her youth. But miraculously, her presence in Alam Dongeng—Mary stumbled over the words—and her rather extensive knowledge of

Western fairy tales and mythical creatures had somehow bridged the way between the two worlds—as evidenced by her own presence here.

"Well then," she said pleasantly, trying to hide all the horrible things she would like to call Garuda behind her smile, "it seems that we need to make good on Garuda's promise and take you to see our land!"

"But she hasn't agreed to help us yet!" Garuda protested.

"You can't force her to do that," Mary said. "Besides, you lied to her, didn't you? You have never seen our world before."

"Our?" Ataneq mused.

"Yes, our." Mary nudged him. "Don't be finicky. It's as much mine as yours."

Mary took Sara's hand and the two humans walked down the path, Ataneq following behind. They walked a long way before Ataneq said they were out of earshot.

"Did they kidnap you, dear?" Mary asked.

"Well, the first time, they did, Aunty. But this time I agreed to come."

"Do you know how to go back?"

Sara shook her head. "Garuda brought me here. I held on to his wing and we kind of disappeared there and reappeared here."

"From where?"

"From my apartment."

"Strange."

"What do you mean?"

"Oh, I don't know anything about your myths or how your realms were set up, but in mine, there is a portal that opens during certain times of the day. It's the only way you can get through from the Old Fairy Kingdom to Britain or vice versa. There's no specific barrier between the Elvish Kingdom and the others, but the paths are guarded by the Elves. I… if I don't leave before midnight, I'll be stuck here until the portal opens the next evening, which I suppose is a good thing for you today. There used to be another way through—not dependent on portals or times—but the Queen's closed it by now. Anyway, I'm sure you don't want to head home that late. Besides, I think someone mentioned you have a young man waiting for you at home?"

Sara blushed. "Yes, but that's mainly because when they kidnapped me the last time, I was gone for four days and everyone was frantic."

"So this time you asked someone to wait for you? Your boyfriend?"

"My manager, actually. And yes, I did. I asked him to wait and if I didn't come back by nightfall, he was to summon Garuda and demand an explanation."

"Good girl."

Ataneq came bounding back down the path. "I think we're home, Mary. The weather's changed."

Mary lifted her head and sniffed the air. "I do think so too." She re-wrapped her shawl around her shoulders. "Oh dear, are you cold?"

Sara was staring fixedly down the path, rubbing her arms. "No, no, I'm not. Is that—is that a dryad?"

Mary turned to see what she was looking at. "Oh yes, that's Euthalia." She waved. "Euthalia! Come here! We have something to show you!"

The dryad soon reached them and was introduced to Sara.

"It's a whole new addition to the Kingdom, Euthalia!" Mary exclaimed. "Have you ever seen the like?"

Euthalia nodded distractedly, her eyes fixed in the distance. "It has happened before—when the Germanic tales were added to the British, and the American ones started to overlap."

"When was that?" Ataneq asked curiously.

"Way before your time, adlet. Though," she turned to look at him, "I'm surprised your world didn't merge with ours when you came."

"It was a different circumstance, I believe," Ataneq murmured bashfully. "I was wandering looking for a new home, and for a way home. Not many of my stories still live, I think."

"But you need to look at the trees, Euthalia. That's what we were calling you for," Mary interjected.

Euthalia looked surprised. "Were you? I didn't hear you."

"Well, we were far in the new forest, and I think they speak a different language, so we weren't sure if the trees there knew you. But why are you here then?"

"The trees," Euthalia said, a wry smile on her lips. "We heard whispers we couldn't understand and we wanted to know what they said."

"We can take you there," Ataneq offered.

Euthalia shook her head. "They might not speak to us if you are there."

"But you wouldn't be able to understand them even if they do."

"I can translate," Sara spoke up.

"But don't you want to see the rest of the Kingdom?" Mary asked.

Sara hesitated. "Well, yes, I do… but…"

Euthalia smiled at her. "Don't worry, my dear. We dryads may not understand, but the trees speak in a language all their own. I'm sure they will understand each other. But we must find out what ails them and we cannot do that with all of you there crowding us." With a smile, she bid them farewell and glided down the path they had come from.

# CHAPTER 7

"So," Mary turned brightly to Sara, "What shall we do now?"

The girl seemed to be looking around, her face a confusion of awe and uncertainty.

"The Court is nearby," Ataneq observed, cricking his neck and looking up at the dark sky nonchalantly.

"And?"

"Your grandmother might be interested…"

Mary shushed him. "Oh, not on the first day, dear. All you'll do is scare the poor thing. She's already so overwhelmed as it is."

"Why would it scare me?" Sara asked.

"My grandmother is a crotchety old thing. She might probably tear your head off. But then again, you're here validly, by invitation—special invitation, mind you—even if you're a little older than she usually expects."

"Older?" The young woman stared blankly at her.

Mary continued on obliviously. "Yes. The humans she tolerates are usually between eight to eighteen. Any younger and they're pests, any older and they're opportunists."

"But… but aren't you human?"

Ataneq laughed. "You missed explaining that part, Mary."

"Oh! I'm sorry. I must have confused you so much. Yes, I'm mostly human. But my grandmother is the Fairy Queen."

"The Fairy Queen!" Sara squeaked.

"You've heard of her?"

"Oh yes, of course. She's in A Midsummer's Night's Dream and Tam Lin—and there's a whole book about her too, I think, though I haven't read that. And isn't she in Peter Pan? Or referred to anyway. And probably in a lot of Enid Blyton. She just… exists."

"I see." Mary wasn't quite sure what she saw. She didn't think it was quite the best decision to show Sara the Court on her very first visit, but she could not think of where else to go. Besides, Mary had always thought the Court the most beautiful part of the Old Fairy Kingdom, especially in the still of the night with the stars twinkling like ethereal fairy lights. She was eager to see if Sara agreed.

Sara's sharp intake of breath as they approached told Mary exactly what she hoped. The old woman smiled to herself.

"It's gorgeous!" Sara gushed.

The Fairy Queen stirred on her throne. "What is this?" she mumbled. It was late, the fae had drunk their fill, scattered across the grass like fallen soldiers.

"A visitor, Grandmother. From Malaysia," Mary added breezily, hoping the faerie would know where it was.

The Queen looked up in interest. "Eh? Where's that?"

Apparently not. "Oh, somewhere quite far away."

"How did she get here?"

"Apparently, we have a new annexe."

This finally roused the Queen fully. "When did that happen?"

"Did you not feel anything, Grandmother?" Mary asked.

"No, I never feel anything, foolish child. It's an addition to my Kingdom, not my body."

"So this has happened before?"

"It happens all the time, in smaller or greater extent, anytime someone is familiar with both worlds."

"Hmm." Mary had to think about that. Something of the sort must have happened in the past sixty years, just that she hadn't been aware of it.

"Of course, someone also has to will it to happen. That doesn't happen as often." The Queen was staring at Sara, a sharp look in her eyes. "So? When did this new addition come about?"

"Today, I would think. At least, we only stumbled upon it—and her—today." Mary looked over to where Ataneq was leading the young woman to meet the Council of Centaurs. Sara seemed quite excited, almost babbling.

"They brought her in?"

Mary nodded. "Special invitation."

"To what end?"

"To save their world, or so I gather."

"All worlds die in time."

"True, grandmother. But not all inhabitants wish to die with it."

"Still, I wonder."

The Fairy Queen rose to her feet and glided over to the young Chinese woman. Sara stopped mid-sentence, blushed and performed something like a mix between a curtsy and a truncated bow.

"Tell your folklore kin that they must abide by my rules or they won't stay long in this land," the Queen said imperiously.

"By… by your rules, your Majesty?"

"Yes, by the rules I have set, which includes—mind you—limitations on the visitation of humans. I'm sure you wouldn't care to be torn limb from limb by an ogre?"

"Oh, oh no, of course not!" Sara stammered.

"Then do let them know."

Mary shook her head as her grandmother left them. Sara stared after her with wide eyes and a small voice, "But what rules are they?"

"Don't you worry, dear. We'll settle it amongst ourselves," Mary said, putting a comforting arm around her shoulder. "Why don't we head somewhere else? Somewhere more pleasant?"

The three of them took their leave of the centaurs, Sara casting one longing glimpse at them.

"I told you it was a bad idea," Mary murmured to Ataneq as they walked.

The adlet smiled wryly. "Well, it had to happen sometime, didn't it?"

They soon left the Court far behind them. As they walked, Mary pointed out the different plants and the different fairy creatures that crossed her path. It reminded her of that day, a long time ago, when her late mother had done the same for her, Jane and their father. Oh, what a terrible—and yet terribly exciting—day that had been! And yet, she wouldn't exchange it for the world. Not when she had gained a whole new world from it. She'd arrived too late to see Jane's show of power, only stumbling in towards the end with the imps and Mr Rowan when Ivy Iliana, her mother, was already quarrelling with the Fairy Queen. Poor Mr Rowan had been green and trembling by then!

Sara was saying something to Ataneq and Mary focused her attention to listen.

"But why don't you want to help them?"

"It's not that I don't want to," Sara said miserably. They sat down by the river. Sara slipped off her slippers and stuck her feet in the cold water. "It's that I don't know how."

"Why not?" Mary asked.

"Because I barely know anything about them!" Her sigh was like a mini breeze of itself. "I didn't grow up with them. I mean, yes, I've heard *of* them. It's hard not to when you grow up in a multi-cultural place like Malaysia. There's an overlap, a passing through. But it's not the same. I grew up with different stories altogether. Stories like these. Places like these. I've dreamed all my life of escaping to a wonder-world like this. All their stories are horrid and gruesome about dead people and dead babies and women being ripped apart and ghosts coming to kill you or haunt you…"

Mary saw Ataneq's eyes flicker to find hers before returning to study Sara's face. Then he deliberately turned his face away and stared into the sky.

"And now they're trusting you to change that for them," he said softly. When she didn't reply, he continued, "I was once supposed to be a child-eater, did you know that? Some stories said that the adlet prowled to catch children unawares, stealing them away from camps to eat them. Some said they guarded children. And encampments. Guess which one I wanted to be?"

"Not all our stories started off pretty, you know," Mary added.

"Yes, I do… but… but I don't want to be the one who appropriates another's culture and changes them into something else. I don't want to be that person."

"Why would you be?"

"Because as much as I am a Malaysian, I am not a Malay! It's not my culture. It's not my stories. It's… difficult."

"Not all those who need voices can find them." Ataneq's reply was so soft that Mary almost missed it.

He cleared his throat and turned to face Sara. "You have this privilege of standing between three worlds. Not many do. Most are confined to one. They struggle to express what they mean in their own language, much less in another language. And here you are—straddling at least two. Maybe three, if I understand you right. Why do you not want this?"

"Because I don't know how. I've always been in one world, excluded by everything else. It feels weird when you say I have access to these other worlds that aren't mine. That don't want me. I'm a stranger in my own land, Ataneq. I'm not wanted."

"Except that now you are."

"I am wanted by figments of my imagination. What if I write everything they want me to and then I get into trouble for it by real world people? I'm not imaginary, as much as I'd like to be. I can't run away and disappear forever."

"You could, if you wanted to."

"But should I?" Sara sighed. She didn't really know why she was making such a fuss. A story was a story was a story, after all. Cultural appropriation was an American issue, not something that any Malaysian really understood. It was all just a silly fuss. Wasn't it? Except it wasn't, not to her anyway, not now, when she was afraid of giving voice to people who might not want her voice to rise above theirs. Had she always been living in fear?

"All stories are important, Sara," Mary said now, holding her hand and rubbing it calmly. Her hands were so soft, so warm. "These ones from your homeland are just as important as the ones you have grown up with. There are so many of our stories out there. There are not enough of yours. Don't you think you should at least try?"

"But it's so hard, Aunty Mary. I don't even know where to start."

"You will, child. Trust your heart. You will know." Mary smiled and rose to her feet. "I think it's time for a late night snack. Are you hungry?"

"Rather." Sara glanced at her watch. It was nearing noon, but the sky had the look of deep night. *Britain,* she reminded herself. *Somewhere behind us on the timezone.*

They made their way to Ataneq's cottage, which was quite near to the stream where they'd been sitting. The adlet fried up some eggs and bacon for them. As they ate, Mary told Sara the story of how she first gained access to the Old Fairy Kingdom. Sara listened in wide-eyed astonishment.

"You saw Smaug?" she said with a tinge of jealousy.

"Yes, I did indeed. He was a large, frightening creature. Very majestic."

"Do you think I'll see him?"

"It depends. He often flies overhead in the mornings and evenings, so there is a chance."

"He won't… eat us, will he?"

"Now you're afraid?" Ataneq teased.

Sara blushed. "A little."

"You're too small for him, dear. He'd rather eat a cow."

Mary yawned. "It's late for me, Sara. I think I'll take a short nap." She got up and walked to the cottage.

Sara looked at Ataneq. "If you need to sleep, that's fine with me," she said.

"I'm fine," he said with a smile.
They sat watching the sun rise as Ataneq told Sara his story.

# CHAPTER 8

It was fully bright when Sara jolted awake. She glanced at her watch. It was nearing seven in the eveneing. She'd been asleep for a little over an hour. Ataneq was still quietly dozing. Mary was standing at the table, making sandwiches.

"Do the seasons here follow Britain?"

Mary shook her head. "Not always. Sometimes it's close, but sometimes it could be the opposite. It really depends. The passage of time isn't always in sync."

"Then how do you know that you'll go home on the same day? What if you go back and find that a bunch of days have passed?"

"Well, that hasn't happened to me yet," Mary said uncertainly. "I just think that the seasons here follow a shorter cycle than that on earth. But the length of the days are the same. Don't you agree, Ataneq?"

Ataneq shook himself and stretched, yawning once as he came out of his slumber. He shrugged non-committally. "I've never really bothered to figure it out."

"We should be heading back to the new kingdom," Mary said. Ataneq nodded and Sara scrambled to her feet. Mary distributed the sandwiches, which they started munching on as they walked.

There was a rustling in the underbrush and Sara looked about nervously. "Nothing's going to attack us, right?"

"Nope. It's probably just the local creatures coming to see who's this new visitor they haven't smelt before."

"You make it sound like I smell."

"You smell like human. It's not something a lot of fairy creatures like," Ataneq said curtly.

"What's that supposed to mean?"

"It's just something we're conditioned against. Not your fault. Nor yours," he said, inclining his head to Mary. "Like a defence mechanism, you know? Fear the predator? Of course, things have changed—are changing. But it doesn't mean you don't need to be cautious."

"But you're kind of in-between. Doesn't that make it easier?" Sara asked.

The adlet snorted. "No. It makes it worse. We're not different enough to be accepted. Not similar enough to be ignored. Hybrids like me and the faun? We're usually the first to be killed in any kind of genocide. Centaurs get it a little better. They've got a long mythology of being wise and dangerous. We're just dangerous… and maybe a little strange."

The rustling became louder. "It's something big, guys," Sara said, looking around nervously.

A dark shadow fell over them. Sara looked up and saw a large hut looming overhead. It seemed to peer at her with its dark, soulless window-eyes and then it jerked a little and headed off to the right.

"Looks like Baba Yaga got wind of you," Mary said. "Let's go see what she wants."

The three headed off in the same direction as the hut, finding that it had settled in a small clearing and was sitting on its haunches. The old lady was coming out of the hut just as they arrived. She was dressed in her usual black, the thin cotton hanging off her skinny frame. Her steel-grey tresses were bunched up in an untidy bun at the back of her head.

"Hmph," Baba Yaga grunted as she looked Sara up and down. "You're not what I expected."

"More riddles, Mother?" Ataneq asked wryly.

"No, not riddles, you silly dog-man. I was told that a great warrior had come to save the world so I came looking for some sort of hero. I should have known to expect that it would all be exaggeration and bunk. They are such a small, weak people."

"Great warrior? Where did you hear that?" Mary asked, perplexed.

"The wind told me there were new people afoot. I went to look out for them and this… queen, I think, of the people told me that a saviour had appeared and she'd gone off to… explore or something. I didn't expect that she'd be with you."

"Oh! We found her quite by chance," Mary replied. "But what did you want with her?"

"To see, of course, who would save us all." Baba Yaga cackled a little as she laughed. "Well, I don't doubt she'll do them a world of good."

"How?"

"Belief is half the battle," the crone replied as she shuffled back into her house.

They watched as the house rose on its feet again and left the clearing.

"What does she mean?" Sara asked, feeling smaller than ever.

Mary and Ataneq exchanged glances.

"Who knows? You'll probably have to figure it out over the next few decades." There was still a tinge of bitterness in Ataneq's voice. If he'd known earlier, if he'd figured out her cryptic words much earlier, who knows what might have happened? He might have been able to go home, to see his sons all grown up, to maybe meet his grandchildren. To see his wife again. But no, he'd taken too long, had lingered too long, forgetting her mission, her question, in his comfortable little cottage in the woods. By the time Jane and Mary had come to shake his world and reveal the answer, it was too late to go home. Still, life had been mostly good for him and he had no complaints.

"We should go," Mary said softly, touching his arm. "Sara needs to go home soon."

He nodded in reply.


The sky grew dark again as they entered the warmth of the rainforest. Sara wondered idly how that worked. How did this fairy land know where one part began and one part ended? Would it always remain this way? Or would the four seasons of the north somehow manage to merge with the heat of the equator? Would that mean that the Old Fairy Kingdom would grow warmer and lose its four seasons? Or would that mean that Alam Dongeng would grow colder? How would the timezones match?

She was a little disappointed that she hadn't managed to see Smaug—the old dragon hadn't flown anywhere near them—or elves—who apparently now kept to their own kingdom—but she'd managed to catch a glimpse of pixies, fairies, goblins, imps, dryads and naiads, besides having met the Fairy Queen, the Centaur Council, Baba Yaga and Ataneq.

A tall figure walked towards them. Sara recognised it as the dryad from earlier in the day. She seemed to be thinking deeply, a frown on her face, almost passing them by until Mary called her by name. Her head shot up then, a smile flickering across her features when her eyes focused on them.

"Did you find out anything?" Mary asked.

"They're dying." Euthalia snorted. "I already knew that one. Of what, I asked. They didn't know. Of lack of interest, one said. I asked if that was possible, but nobody knew. It's as if their collective brains have switched off. It was so difficult to talk to them. They didn't know who I was! At any rate, did you have a good time?"

"Oh yes!" Sara replied enthusiastically. "It was lovely."

"I'm glad. Do come over often."

Euthalia followed them as they headed back to the same clearing where Mary and Ataneq had found Sara with the Malaysian fairy folk. The clearing was quiet now—most of them had dispersed, leaving only Garuda waiting with the Raja and Permaisuri Bunian.

The atmosphere was a little tense and awkward, with the seven of them staring at each other mutely. As the sky grew darker, strange figures seemed to take shape in the trees overhead and around them. Sara could feel her muscles tensing, the little she knew of the Toyol and the Pontianak and various kinds of ghosts coming to mind. She gripped Mary's hand tightly.

Mary looked around at the gathering shapes, a small frown coming to her face. "Huh," she exclaimed softly. "I see what you mean."

"They have come to meet you too, Penglipur Lara," Permaisuri Bunian said, holding her hand out towards Sara. "You need to tell their stories too."

"But I don't like horror stories," Sara protested. "I… I can't."

"Then tell the stories of their innocence," a new voice said loudly, startling everyone. They looked around, trying to see who had spoken. The little deer from before appeared from the bushes.

"Sang Kancil," Raja Bunian bent his head in acknowledgement. "It is good to see you here."

"Your counsel is welcome, O greatest of all mouse deer," Garuda said, throwing his wings wide in welcome.

The mouse deer inclined his head. "Well met, O Raja Bunian, Permaisuri Bunian, Garuda. And our new friends—welcome."

"We saw you this morning, did we not?" Ataneq said as he made the introductions.

"Yes, that was me. I was afraid that you would not understand what I was indicating to you this morning. But I am glad that you did."

"So you *were* herding us here!" Mary exclaimed.

"Yes, I was. Those monkeys are terrible. They're always causing trouble. I didn't want them to cause you any further problems and thought it best to send you this way. You seemed the most likely people to be able to assist our young saviour here." He smiled at Sara.

Sara didn't know what to do or what to think. It was awful that everyone thought of her as some sort of saviour, or some sort of magical creature who would somehow save their land. As she saw it, they were the magical creatures with the powers, whilst she was just a simple girl who would like very much to go home in one piece. On the same day.

"I'm sorry to have to disappoint you, Sang Kancil," she spoke up now. Someone had to disabuse them of that strange notion! "I really doubt that I can help."

"But you already have! This connection—this joining of our land to the Old Fairy Kingdom—is fantastic! I already see all kinds of opportunities." His eyes twinkled with excitement. "I'm sure whatever you write or do will be a great help in the future, but what you have done here is already astounding. I've met with very helpful people already. Thank you."

"Uh, you're welcome?" Sara couldn't mask the doubt in her voice. The creatures of the night were already starting to come out from their places amongst the trees, closing in to catch a glimpse of Sara and the other newcomers. She shivered a little. She wasn't usually afraid of ghost stories, but seeing strange figures approaching in the dark wasn't a very pleasant sight.

"Don't be afraid," Sang Kancil said. "They won't harm you. They want you to hear their stories. Some of them are quite tragic, really."

"But don't they eat people? Or murder them? Drink their blood?"

"Don't vampires do the same?" Sang Kancil said pointedly.

"I don't like vampires either."

"Ah, well." The mouse deer made a shrug-like gesture. "It is getting late. And you are tired. I think it is time that you go home. You can come again another day, or who knows? We might visit you."

On those ominous words, Sang Kancil disappeared into the night. Garuda approached Sara now, extending his wing again.

"Well then, it has been great meeting you. I hope I can do so again," Sara said, extending a hand to Mary. The old woman embraced her instead. Ataneq shook her hand next, followed by Euthalia. Waving goodbye, she took a hold of Garuda. Just as the world disappeared around them, Mary shouted, "Write to me, Sara! Search for Mary Hays!"

The fairy world faded from Sara's sight and hearing.

# CADENZA

The woman that comes to see him isn't the Lang Suir. She's old. Bent. Grey-haired. Foreign.

"What do you want?" he asks, speaking the language of his colonial past. They master him and his kin no more, but still, he must bow.

"To understand." Her speech is equally as accented. Neither of them are native to this language, but they make do, as they have always done. A bitter meeting ground.

"Where do you come from?" He knows, but he must have confirmation. He must always seek confirmation, though it tears his heart apart.

"From the myth." She frowns. "As do you. Can you not return?"

He shakes his head. "Not without invitation."

"I would invite you."

"But you have no right."

The old woman nods. "Why does he hate you?"

He sighs, feeling the years he has spent on this earth more than the years he has spent in his home. *Not my home*, he reminds himself a thousand thoughts too late. *I am human.* This *is my true home.* He shakes his head ruefully. He feels no need to clarify who she means. There can only be one *he* in this conversation.

"I would have been him, you know? I could have been king, changeling that I am, had I not found my love in this world. But even if I had not found her, I would have let him be king. It was his birthright, though he believes me not. Our fa—our late father would have it no other way." Strange to think of the old Bunian dead. Death comes to us all, natural or not.

"So he threw you out. In jealousy."

"I ran. Before he could." He waits, eyes lowered, for the recrimination. Eventually, he raises his gaze again and asks, "Why are you here?"

"Because Baba Yaga smells war on the horizon. And you are the centrepiece of it all."

# CHAPTER 9

Helmi looked at the clock for the umpteenth time. It was still only half past nine in the evening. He continued pacing the living room, anxious. Ever since Sara had left that morning, he'd been worrying about her. He'd been too restless to relax, so he'd gone in to the office to finish up some work. As if there were nothing else to occupy him on a Saturday morning.

Xiu Li had leaned against the door frame of his office, a smirk on her face.

"What?" he'd asked harriedly.

"You like her, don't you?"

"No. Why?" Still, there had been that twist in his gut he refused to acknowledge.

"You wouldn't be so worried about anyone else."

"No one else has been kidnapped by fairy creatures."

"Your point being?"

"It's different. You don't know what these creatures are like. How blood-thirsty they are. You don't play with spirits, Xiu Li. It's not safe."

"So if sweet Aminah were to disappear into fairyland you'd be equally as worried?"

"Aminah? What would Aminah have to do with those things?"

"Nothing. I was just saying."

Helmi had shaken his head. "Xiu Li, I'm not in the mood. This isn't fun and games. It's dangerous. I'm justly worried."

Xiu Li had snorted. "Yeah right. And I'm a princess."

He hadn't stopped for dinner—just packed some food along with him and headed straight to Sara's apartment. The guard nodded as he drove in—obviously too well known by now; he had to think about that soon—but he hadn't stopped to think about it too much. That had been at seven.

Two and a half hours later, he was still waiting. He tried to quieten his nerves and his limbs. Still two and a half hours to midnight. She would come back in time. She had to. Nine-thirty-five. He sat down, opened his book to where his bookmark was and started reading. Nine-forty. He looked back down at his novel, eyes scanning the same paragraph. He shut the book and went back to pacing.

"Helmi?"

He sat up with a jolt. When had he fallen asleep? Sara bent over him, shaking him by the shoulder. "You're back! When did—" He glanced up at the clock. It was ten-fifty. He'd been asleep for half an hour.

"Just."

"And everything… was okay? You're alright?"

"Oh, it was wonderful, Helmi. Garuda was a big fat liar, but—but it was great."

She settled onto the couch next to him, leaning just slightly into his side, rambling a little as she told him about her day.

"Sang Kancil was there? You met Sang Kancil?" he exclaimed when she fell silent with a smile on her lips.

"Yes! It was awesome. You should come next time."

"Would they let me?"

"I don't know. Why not?"

"It feels like there are a lot of rules to being in this place. Especially after what the Fairy Queen said."

Sara nodded. "Maybe. But I'm sure we can work something out."

There was a brief silence. Helmi stared at his fingers, laced together on his lap, trying to ignore the warmth of Sara leaning against him. She shifted away. He looked up.

"Uh, so I was wondering if you could probably tell me a little more about Malay folklore? I mean, I haven't actually agreed to help yet, but I figured knowing more wouldn't hurt, kan? I mean, if I knew more I could probably help better?"

"You want me to tell you stories?"

"Well, if you know any. Or maybe find me some books."

Helmi didn't know if he should laugh or cry. This could either be the perfect way to get to know Sara better—outside of work—or it could be a disaster. "Look, I'm not good at telling stories. I could probably find you some kids books, I don't know. I think my parents have thrown all of them out or given them to people. But I can try. They're most likely only in Malay though."

"What's wrong with that?"

There was a quick quirk in his lips as he said, "Do you even read Malay?"

Sara rolled her eyes. "Of course I do! I didn't spend eleven years of my life learning it to not be able to read it."

He spread his hands, palms out, in what he hoped was a conciliatory gesture. "I have to ask, you know. So many Chinese get upset when you speak to them in Malay."

"Those are the Chinese-Educated ones." She paused. "I don't like them either."

"Really?" It seemed something Sara was rather passionate about but he didn't know how to ask more about it without seeming a little racist. Luckily, she continued on her own.

"Yeah. They're weird. Like… you're Malaysian for goodness' sake. Not some mainland Chinese person. You don't have to act all affronted because I don't speak Chinese. I'm not from China. I don't understand them."

"Right. Anyway, I'll go try to dig up some old books."

"I suppose all this wouldn't have happened if our parents had actually continued telling us their own stories." She seemed to be blushing. "Or if we'd cared enough to listen."

Helmi shrugged. "People change. Things change. Culture changes. What of it?"

"Don't you care if your folktales disappear like that?"

"I… I don't know, Sara. It's not a big deal to me. I don't read that much. I mean, I work. I get money. If I have time, I'll read a book. If not, I'll watch TV."

"You don't watch local television, do you?"

"Not really," he admitted.

"See?"

"See what? Local shows are crappy. They're all about star-crossed lovers and people who try to jinx others by getting a bomoh to curse them."

"And all international shows are about star-crossed lovers and people who backstab them in the office to get ahead."

He wagged a finger at her. "No, they have superhero movies too."

"We have Cicakman," she retorted.

"Did you even watch that show?"

"Actually, no. But I heard about it."

"It was… weird."

She giggled, leaning against him again. It felt good. The warmth of her body and the beating of her heart calmed his anxious soul. He sighed.

She turned her head slightly to look at him. "What was that for?"

"Nothing. Just… thankful."

"For?"

"That you're here. And you're safe."

"Thanks for looking out for me."

"Anytime." It didn't feel like the right time to say anything else and Helmi didn't want to push his luck, so he slowly got to his feet and started packing up his things.

He straightened up, slinging his backpack over his right shoulder. "So, I'll see you on Monday?"

"Yes, boss. I'll be on time for work."

He grinned at her. "I wasn't going to say that."

"Sure you were. You were going to say that I'm always late for work and I'd better buck up." She grinned back.

"No, actually, what I was going to say was would you like to come over tomorrow?" Was he really? But he'd said it now.

"Come over to where?"

"My house."

"For what?"

"To look for old books. That's what you wanted, kan?" Her look of incredulity surprised him. "What, you don't think I have any?"

"No, no…" she stammered. "It's just that you've never invited anyone home before."

"How would you know?"

"Uh, Mi, we're girls. We gossip."

He didn't know what to say. "Uh, well, take it as you will," he tried to keep it ambiguous, "but I'm just saying that if you want, you can come over and see what you can find. I can't guarantee you'll find anything, but maybe my mom would have stories to share." That was what she had wanted, wasn't it?

"Sure… sure. I…" Sara seemed a little stumped.

"You can let me know tomorrow." His hand tightened around his bag strap, wondering if this was a good or a bad move. "Early, if possible. So my mum can cook more for dinner."

"Oh, oh sure."

"Eh, but she overcooks anyway." Helmi was sure he was being too desperate by now. "Anyway. See you tomorrow."

He headed to the door, Sara trailing a little after him.
"I'll see you tomorrow, Mi."
He headed home in a cloud of anticipation.

# COUNTERPOINT

He thinks he's dreaming, but maybe he's not. It feels like something else. A vision, maybe, though he hasn't had those in years.

The Lang Suir is there, and *him. Aria.* He shakes his head in confusion. That cannot be. Why would Aria consort with the enemy? Why would the Lang Suir attempt to court him if she were already in league with Aria? They are talking, but he cannot hear what they say. It's not a vision then—what use would a vision be if it gave him no clues to the future?

He watches as the pair stare each other down, their movements wary. They remind him of a pair of fighting spiders. Hidden in the leaves, captured and pitted against each other. But who is pitting who against who? Nothing makes sense. Aria says something, his face hard and unrelenting. The Lang Suir clenches her fist, and then she nods. A deal seems to have been struck, but he still can't tell what it is.

The scene changes abruptly, sending waves of dizziness over him. He watches as Aria argues with his father—a vision of the past then? A seeing?—and storms out, seeking his wife, Nur. The two of them sit and plot, though he still doesn't know what about. Maybe this is all the Lang Suir knows. Maybe she can't hear them either. Why is she showing him this?

Aria slips something—crushed leaves? A powder? He can't quite tell—into his father's food. Nur opens the door—

—And he sees. He understands how an immortal Bunian can die. How their defences could have been weakened so. Why he had to go.

The dream slips away, and the last thing he sees is the Lang Suir. She looks directly at him and nods.

He understands now that he must go back. Somehow.

# CHAPTER 10

"So this is your friend," Helmi's mother said enthusiastically as Sara kicked off her shoes and stepped into the house. "We have heard so much about you, Sara."

"It's good to meet you, Aunty…"

"Dina," she supplied.

"Aunty Dina."

"And this is my husband, Rashid."

Sara greeted him in turn.

"We heard you have been having trouble with some spirits," Dina said as they entered the living room.

Sara frowned a little, wondering how much Helmi had said, before nodding. Well, she *had* asked him for help, and presumably his parents would be the ones who could help.

Helmi's father sat on the three-seater couch in the middle of the room, gesturing for her to take a seat on the two-seater opposite him. Sara sat down, and at his prompting, started to tell him briefly about the encounter with the Orang Bunian and Garuda, as well as her trip into Alam Dongeng. Dina came back into the room, bearing a tray of cold drinks, followed closely behind by Helmi, who was laden with a tray of kuih and snacks.

"You are blessed to be taken notice of by the spirits! I have long wanted to see that magical world myself," Rashid said. "My father used to regale us with story after story of the fairy world. He's out right now, but really, if you came for Dongeng, you should be asking him."

They talked a little on inconsequential things after that, asking after her family (her parents were fine, they lived in another state) and talking a little about Helmi's younger brother and his family. Sara hadn't realised until then that Helmi was the elder of the two. She had heard of his brother before, seen pictures of his nieces, but had always thought that the married brother was older.

After a while, Dina excused herself to continue cooking. Rashid followed Helmi and Sara to the tiny store room.

"It's a bit messy, I'm afraid. We haven't looked at most of these for a long time! Not since the boys grew up," he apologised.

"It's fine, uncle," Sara said, staring at the musty boxes. "Are all of these books?"

Helmi laughed. "No, no. Not all of them. Just these here." He pointed to two boxes that had been pushed aside. "If all of them were books, we'd be here forever! I'm afraid we don't read that much."

Sara opened the top of one of the boxes, finding that it was quite full. "How come none of these went to your nieces?"

"Hah. My brother would rather buy them new books. Those fancy colourful ones on sale at Big Bad Wolf. They don't like these old stories, especially since they're all in Malay."

"Oh?" Her brow wrinkled in confusion.

"They mainly speak English at home now," Helmi said with a shrug.

The books were old and musty, with that distinctive smell of old paper mixed with dust. Sara pulled a few titles randomly out of the box and flipped through them, throwing up a cloud of dust, making them cough.

"I'll get a cloth." A short while later, Helmi came back with two pieces of damp cloth. "Let's take everything out and wipe them down before we sort through them," he said.

Sara nodded in agreement, her arm over her nose and mouth to keep out the fine, tickling powder. Sitting side by side, they started working.


Dina had whipped up a feast. There was deep fried chicken and an exquisite fish curry, turmeric-fried cabbage and sambal-fried kangkung, as well as some mutton rendang. Sara was astonished at the amount of food on the table, seeing that there were only five of them.

"I told you my mother overcooks," Helmi said, earning himself a light slap on his shoulder from his mother.

"It all looks so delicious!" Sara exclaimed. It had been a long while since Sara had experienced a home-cooked meal, and she enjoyed it thoroughly. Even more than that, she enjoyed the friendly banter and gentle ribbing that took place over the dining table between Helmi, his parents and grandfather, and the warm way they drew her in to their conversation.

Sara was stuffed by the end of dinner. She leaned back in her chair, looking at all the leftovers with regret.

"Do you want to take some home?" Dina asked.

"Oh, there's no need, Aunty Dina. I have no idea when I will be able to eat it."

"Surely tomorrow for dinner, or something?"

"Come on, Sa. Take some home. You'll make her really happy."

Reluctantly, she gave in. At least she wouldn't have to think about what to eat tomorrow. Or the day after, judging by the portions that Dina was now packing for her.

"That's really too much for one person," she protested faintly.

"Oh, I doubt so. It will be finished in no time," Dina said, ignoring her protest.

Once they had packed the food away, Sara got up and offered to help wash up, but Dina shooed her away. "I'm sure you and Helmi have things to do. Rashid can help me."

Her husband started to protest, but Dina pulled him along with her to the kitchen and Helmi led her back to the store room. Checking that there was no one around, Helmi turned to Sara sheepishly and apologised.

"What for?"

"My parents made it really awkward, didn't they?"

Sara shrugged as she laid another book aside. "Parents are parents. They're natural at being awkward." She paused with a book in her hand, looking at him inquisitively. "Do they think I'm your girlfriend?"

"Uhh…"

"Tell me frankly, please."

"They think I like you," he managed to say almost nonchalantly.

"And you gave them that impression because?"

"Because…" He sat back and stared at her. "Sa, I'd wanted to bring it up in a better time, a better place. But I guess there's no better place and time than the present, huh? Especially since my family has already spilt all the beans." He cleared his throat nervously. "Would you be my girlfriend?"

She stared at him mutely. Her cheeks felt hot, flushed.

"I mean, it's alright if you say no. I… I didn't think…" He stopped when he saw her lips move. He leaned nearer, trying to make out what she said so silently.

"Yes, I think," was her quiet whisper.

His hand reached over to hers and they clasped in the dimness of the dusty store room.

"You'll have to save me from the spirits, you know."

"I know."

They finished up wiping the last few books and then started to tackle the difficult business of choosing which books would be the most useful. The first thing Sara did was put back the Malay translations of Enid Blyton, saying that she knew enough about those. She was rather surprised to see such a huge amount of those. She supposed that they had been popular back then.

That left her with several English translations of Malay folktales in really difficult English, and several old tomes in Malay. "I suppose I should start with these," she said glumly.

"Why the face?" Helmi asked.

"They don't actually look very interesting. I suppose it's the weird covers."

"I thought you liked old books."

"I do! It's just… I don't know." She picked up the five books and put them into her backpack. "I suppose I'd better be getting home."

"When did you start dealing in dark arts, adik?" The growling voice startled both Helmi and Sara.

# CHAPTER 11

"Dark arts? What do you mean?" Sara asked.

"Atuk? What's this about?" Helmi asked his grandfather.

Abdul Mansoor ignored him. "Where did you get him?"

She looked around, confused. "Who? Helmi? The books?"

"That toyol! They're not to be played with, adik. Where did you get him?" He spoke with urgency, a ferocity in his voice that scared her.

"Pakcik, I don't know what you're talking about."

"I see him now, clinging to your back."

She twisted her head about, trying to see what he was talking about, but all she saw was empty air behind her. And yet, there was an ache in her shoulder, now that he mentioned it.

"Pakcik, whatever it is you're seeing, I swear, I don't know anything about it. I haven't done anything at all!"

"Have you had any strange dreams? Any weird happenings in your house?"

Sara gaped at him. There *had* been something. She'd dismissed it as a dream, snuggled in her blanket, curled around her bolster. It was just a little thing. The image of a child playing in the corner of her room. She'd opened her eyes wider to look, but there was nothing there. She'd only been dreaming. But as she closed her eyes again, she could hear a soft singing in the distance. Peeking through her half-closed lids, she again saw something like a small child playing in the corner of the room, but when she opened her eyes, there was nothing. She was sure she'd dreamt the whole thing up.

Abdul Mansoor folded his arms and frowned. "It seems that the spirits are taking things further. I think you should talk to Garuda and ask him why they are attacking you."

"What is it, pakcik? What kind of spirit is it?"

He looked surprised. "Do you not know what a Toyol is?"

She shook her head sheepishly. "I've heard of it before, but I have no idea what it is or what it looks like."

"It's a child-like spirit, something like what you described seeing last night. A toddler. They can be benevolent when they're not attached to a human. This one… I am not sure if he is attached to you or he is just stalking you… so I do not know if he will turn violent or not. Toyols live on blood or raw meat. They suck blood to survive, so if this one decides it belongs to you, it will start drinking your blood. Once they are attached, they do not ever leave. It will be yours for life—and to your children and grandchildren's lives."

"How-how do I get rid of it?"

"It is very difficult. Try to make sure it does not attach itself to you."

"How do I do that?"

"The fact that you can't see it is good—for you. It means it is not yet yours. Maybe it will go away of its own accord when it gets bored. It is possible that the Toyol is just attracted to the spark of magic that now shrouds you after your trip to Alam Dongeng. The spirits are very sensitive to this field. As am I. You don't see it, but there are many spirits in this area, all watching you."

"Are they dangerous? Will they harm her?" Helmi asked.

"There is some modicum of protection around her," Abdul Mansoor replied. "The same magic field that attracts them also protects her from their evils."

"Did Garuda do this on purpose? Does he know what he's done?"

"I'm not sure. That is a question you must ask him yourself. Whether it was done unwittingly, or whether he has a darker plan, I do not know. I just know this—you must be on your guard, Sara Liew. I believe the Orang Bunian do not mean harm to you, but dabbling in the spirit world always comes with danger. Maybe you should ask for their protection."

Sara nodded. "I'll… I will talk to them about it." *And I really should talk to Aunty Mary as well,* she thought. *Maybe she would know what to do. If I can find her.*

"Do you have marbles?"

"Marbles? Why?"

"Putting little play things in your house—marbles, beads, beans—will also help to distract the Toyol so that they will forget any mischief that they or others may have been planning against you."

"Marbles no, but I do have some beads. What do I do with them?"

"Hang them on your door post." He seemed to think a while. "Probably near the windows as well, in case they are being lured by your flying friend."

"Do you really think Garuda could be doing this to me on purpose?"

"Who knows? The thoughts of magical beings are hard to decipher." His face crinkled into an unexpectedly wistful smile. "Ah, to be there again."

"Atuk? You've never mentioned that you could see the spirit realm. When I asked—when I asked for help, why did you refer me to Pakcik Rozaimi instead?"

Abdul Mansoor froze, a strange look on his face. "You talked about the Orang Bunian. Rozaimi can talk to them but I am closed off from them forever." He turned sharply and left the room.


Her house seemed a little empty and cold after the warmth of having been in a family house once again. Sara put the food packages in the fridge, dumped the books on her bed and went to take a bath. Then she turned her drawers out looking for the beads she was sure she had. She found some, but they weren't exactly what she remembered. She strung them up on her door, wondering if she was just being a bit paranoid.

"Better safe than sorry," she mumbled to herself as she went to her kitchen to make herself a cup of Milo. She figured that something warm and chocolaty would help to calm her nerves.

She brought her mug into her room, setting it on her bedside table as she crawled into bed and pulled the covers around her. Snug, she picked up the topmost book and started reading. A noise at the window caught her attention and she turned her head slowly to look. From the corner of her eye, she could see a figure tapping at the beads, looking very distracted. It was a child, as Abdul Mansoor had described. But as she peered closer at it, she noted that it looked a little greenish, as if it were sick. She quickly looked away, trying to slow her rapid breath. She didn't want to attract its attention.

Sipping on her drink, she tried to continue reading, but couldn't get past the next few sentences. Her eyes kept slipping to the side to look at the Toyol. At one point, the little thing yawned, showing her a full mouth of sharp teeth. In the end, she gave up. She closed the book, turned off her light and pulled the blankets over her head. Maybe if she fell asleep, it would go away. At least it wasn't asking her for blood or making her eat raw meat, as her quick search on Wikipedia earlier had confirmed.

Sara slept badly, tossing and turning in her sleep. In her dreams, she saw all manner of creatures, all clamouring for her attention. The Toyol tugged at the hem of her dress, asking her to adopt him. A tall ghost with extremely long arms and legs sat disconsolately at the bottom of her bed, asking to be released. When she looked in the distance, the light of a candle passed back and forth, carried by yet another ghost.

A Pontianak appeared by her bed, pale in the moonlight, her long, black hair covering her face. And then she looked up, revealing her dark eyes and her hungry mouth. "Why do you ignore us, Penglipur Lara? Why do you let us die?"

"No! No, I do not!"

"Why do you ignore us? Listen to us!"

"What is it you want?"

"Save us. Lay us to rest. Lay us to rest."

"How?"

Sara woke up, covered in sweat, her eyes swollen with tears. "I... I cannot. I cannot," she said over and over again as she rocked herself on the bed, her arms around her knees.

But now they were there around her, even with her eyes open. The Hantu Galah at the foot of her bed, the Hantu Kum-kum leering at her and lusting after her blood. There was a scratching at the window and she didn't dare look. One of the creatures opened it—she could feel the warm air coming in and mixing with the cold air-conditioning—and there was the sound of talons scraping on wood. She looked up, hoping that Garuda had come to save her. Instead, an owl perched at the head of her bed, glaring with bright yellow eyes. An oily shadow detached itself from the far end of the room and lurched towards her. She screamed, closing her eyes and rocking herself again.

She'd wanted to live in a land of fairy creatures. She'd wanted to help fairy folk. Instead she was surrounded by nightmares and she couldn't find her way out. Her fumbling fingers found her phone.

# ADAGIO

He goes to the one person he thinks can help.

The bomoh shakes his head. "I can't *make* them see you, you know," he says. "It's not an enchantment I know how to break."

"But Aria—"

"Can't be reasoned with. I know I've tried. He threatened me too. And I *have* asked on your behalf. You're barred, on pain of death. You don't want to die, do you?"

He hesitates. "If I die there, they won't even have a body to bury here."

"You can't do that to your family."

He paces. "No, I can't. What do I do, Rozaimi?"

Rozaimi looks into the distance.

He wonders if the bomoh is talking to the unseen Bunians, if they would linger here in this house now that he is in it. He wonders if any of them would still acknowledge him and talk to him for friendship's sake, but he's fairly sure that none will. The Raja—no matter who held the title—has always held too strong a sway.

It's late and he should go, should leave his friend in peace, but Rozaimi doesn't say anything so neither does he.

They sit in the living room in silence until Rozaimi suddenly gets up and opens the door.

Helmi enters, flustered and bewildered.

# CHAPTER 12

The incessant ringing annoyed Helmi. He glanced at the clock. Who would call him at three in the morning? The ringing stopped. Good. He rolled over to go back to sleep. It started ringing again. He reached over and grabbed the phone, ready to chew out the caller, when he realised that it was Sara. Hurriedly, he answered. Her sentences were incoherent, garbled, interrupted with sobs and deep breaths. He tried to get her to calm down, and she would subside a little, only to start crying again.

"Stay with me, Sa. Stay with me. I'm coming over." He put her on the speaker as he hurriedly changed out of his pyjamas and ran out to the car. With no traffic on the road, it only took him fifteen minutes to reach her place, speeding most of the way.

"Open the door, Sara, I'm here. I'm here," he said into the phone soothingly. There were noises in the apartment and the door flung open. Helmi took her in his arms, crooning and whispering into her ear. Slowly, he manoeuvred her back into the house, closing and locking the door behind him. Bit by bit, he got the story from her in between sobs and gasps for air as they cuddled on the couch.

"It'll be fine, Sara. It will all be fine. We'll talk to Garuda, get him to place some protections on this place. We'll be very firm with him. No more horror stories in the middle of the night. Shh. Hush." He led her back to bed and tucked her in, pulling a chair over to sit beside it. Each time she stirred and whimpered, he reached over and patted her shoulder, soothing her back to sleep.

He woke with a crick in his neck. Slowly, he leaned forward, rubbing his neck, and wondering why he'd fallen asleep in a chair. Hadn't he gone to bed properly last night? He froze when he realised that he wasn't in his room. The clock on the night stand beside him blinked that it was 5:47 in bright red lights. The bed in front of him was empty. He closed his eyes again, memories of this morning's events filtering into his subconscious. He opened his eyes. The bed was still empty. Where was she?

"Sara?" he called softly. Maybe she'd gone to the washroom. But the adjoining toilet door stood ajar and it was dark inside. The bedroom door was similarly open so he got up, stretched his aching muscles, and went to look.

The rest of the one-roomed apartment was dark. He went to check the couch and found that no one was sleeping on it. A sense of strangeness came over him. The main door was still locked from the inside, the deadbolt tightly closed. He remembered doing that last night. There was no way she'd be able to go out and lock the deadbolt from the outside.

"Sa?" he called again, louder this time. Was she hiding from him? Why would she hide from him? Was she having a psychotic breakdown? He walked around the apartment again, as if trying to see where Sara was hiding. She wasn't anywhere. Heading back to the bedroom, he checked the washroom, wondering if she'd fallen in there. It was empty. A slight flutter caught his attention. His eyebrows started to furrow as he headed to the window. It was wide open. He drew the curtains back, allowing the faint light from outside to stream in as real fear gripped his heart for the first time.

*Had she? But why would she? It didn't make sense. She couldn't have. She wouldn't have.*

A loud sound pierced his ear drums and for a moment, he thought that it was the siren of a fire engine. Two seconds later, he realised that it was Sara's alarm going off. He crossed the room to her bed, picked up her handphone and switched off the alarm. It was six.

Heading back to the window, he leaned out as far as he dared to see if he could see anything outside. The angle was too awkward and he was too high up to see the ground, but he could hear a commotion. With fear in his heart, he grabbed both their phones, scrabbled in her handbag for the house keys and dashed out the door.

*It's not her. Not her. She wouldn't do that. Would she? No.*

He stabbed at the lift button repeatedly, his head swivelling to look at the fire escape. But no, the lift was almost here. It would definitely be faster than if he ran, though he couldn't keep still. The little ding of the lift made him jump. He dashed into the lift, startling the bleary-looking couple inside with their young child.

"Do you know what's happening downstairs?" he asked.

They shook their heads. He couldn't stand still, his feet tapping a rhythm all the way to the ground. When the lift doors finally opened, he dashed out, heading to the direction Sara's window had faced. The commotion grew louder as he got nearer. Soon he could see a sizable crowd gathered around what looked like a body on the ground.

"What happened?" he asked as he pushed his way forward. The returned word *suicide* echoed in his head. His heart sank. *No, no, no, no, no! How could this happen?*

"Sara?" he called as he got nearer to the front. "Sa?" The crowd started to part before him, letting him dash forward to the sprawled body. He could feel the bile in his throat, that lump in his chest and in his belly. The weakness in his legs. He reached her.

And blinked.

It wasn't her.

"Alhamdulilah," he whispered under his breath. A cry came up from somewhere else, some other people were pushed to the front, running over and screaming over the body.

But Helmi had sunk to his feet, relief and worry washing over him in alternating waves. It wasn't her. But where was she? He looked up at the apartment. High above him, he could see the curtains billowing out of an open window. As the sun rose and the light grew stronger, the beads—so small he couldn't see them—glinted, flashing like fire in the sun.

*Garuda.*


Helmi went to work methodically. First, he called in a family emergency for himself, barely remembering to record another leave application for Sara. Emergency or medical? He couldn't decide. Emergency sounded better. He didn't know where to get a medical cert for her. Then he went home and took a long, cold shower. Feeling a little more refreshed, he sat down for breakfast, vaguely replying to his parents that he'd gone for an early morning walk.

He left the house trying to look calm, his backpack slung on his right shoulder. Inside, Garuda's feather was stuck in between the pages of his notebook. He wondered if his mother would realise that food was missing from the fridge. It didn't matter. She probably assume he'd been hungry. Then he'd driven to Rozaimi's house.

Rozaimi opened the door before he knocked. He was surprised to see his grandfather there.

"What happened?" Abdul Mansoor surged to his feet upon seeing Helmi.

"She's missing. Do you know—" Helmi looked helplessly at Rozaimi, but the bomoh shook his head.

"I have heard nothing from the Orang Bunian."

Helmi groaned. He ran a hand through his tousled hair.

Abdul Mansoor pushed him to sit on the couch. "Tell us what you know."

Helmi hesitated. It felt awkward, telling this story, with his grandfather looking on—what would he think? What would his *mom* think?—but he swallowed. Abdul Mansoor's eyes were shrouded, masking his emotions. He stayed silent when Helmi finished recounting his story.

"You were there?" Rozaimi asked Helmi again, his eyes worried.

"I fell asleep."

"But you were in the room."

"Yes," Helmi replied rather reluctantly. He didn't want to give the wrong impression.

All Rozaimi did was mutter enchantments, more to himself than to Helmi or his grandfather. Rozaimi grabbed a bag from his room, spoke something softly to his wife, and then the three men piled into Helmi's car. The ride was short and very silent.

Sara's apartment was just as Helmi had left it. The window still stood open, the curtain billowing out in the wind with the beads caught in a corner. Rozaimi looked at it with a frown.

"Was the window open when you slept?"

Helmi tried to remember. "I don't think so. Yeah, the air-conditioning was on, so the window was probably closed."

"But you did not check. With your eyes."

Helmi shook his head. "She was already in a panicked state when I came over. It… it didn't seem important."

The old man was mumbling under his breath. Helmi couldn't make out exactly what it was, but it sounded as if he were chanting a prayer. A shiver ran through his spine.

"Look. I've still got Garuda's feather. I'm going to call him and make him answerable for this."

"The dark spirits did this. Garuda may help you find her, may help you champion her, but he did not do this."

"He started it!"

"When a landslide happens do you blame the soil that falls? Or do you blame the men that uprooted the trees?"

"What?"

"Be careful where you put the blame, young Helmi. Especially with a powerful being like Garuda. One who may bear you more harm than good if he puts himself against you."

Abdul Mansoor stayed silent. He stood by the window in Sara's room, looking out at the distant mountains. There was a smattering of clouds on the horizon.

Helmi struggled to bring his emotions under control. He could feel panic rising in every fibre of his being, fear oozing out of his pores, and anger bubbling inside his chest. He took a deep breath, exhaling slowly, counting until ten, until fifteen, until his breath ran out. "Do the Orang Bunian tell you anything?"

Rozaimi shook his head. "They are not here, Helmi. They do not enter a house unwelcome. All there is here is the lingering of a nightmare. It does not tell me anything but that they have left this physical realm. Call Garuda if you wish. Maybe he will know something."

Helmi nodded. Rozaimi and Helmi returned to the kitchen. Helmi took out Garuda's feather carefully and placed it on the table. Unable to find any matches or lighters, he brought it over to the stove and set it aflame. Neither of them noticed when Abdul Mansoor closed Sara's door quietly.

A bright flash of light blinded the two men. When Helmi could see again, the flaming bird-form of Garuda was perched on one of Sara's kitchen chairs.

Garuda looked around the room with disdain. "What is it, young man? Why do you call me now? I do not have your young woman with me."

Helmi's mouth opened and closed silently as he tried to form words through his indignance.

"Well, say something. Before I lose my patience."

Rozaimi came to the rescue. "Oh great Bird of all Birds, we do not call you for fun. The young Sara is missing—has been missing—since the early hours of this day. I have tried to find her with my magics— what little of it that I have—but all I know is that the people of the night have come calling for her and have taken her. Where to, we do not know. O majestic Garuda, fire-bird of glory, would you please help us to find her?"

Garuda preened a little at the old man's solicitous words. Then his face grew serious. "What do you mean missing?"

Helmi repeated the sequence of the morning's events, the bird nodding at every other sentence.

"You did well to call me," he said in the end.

"You can help us?" Helmi asked hopefully.

"We will call the Orang Halus to our aid. Come with me, Helmi. We must rally the forces of good to search for our Penglipur Lara. I do not know why these Hantu have come against her, but once we find them, and her, we will know." He stopped and seemed to think for a while. "The Hantu rarely ever work together, unlike the Orang Halus. I am curious to know what has caused them to take this drastic course of action." The bird cocked his head to the left and looked at Helmi. "Are you ready?"

Helmi swallowed and nodded. "What do we do? Do we fly like you did the last time with Sara?"

Garuda smiled. "The fairies your girlfriend has brought us into contact with has taught us much. We do not need to fly between worlds anymore. We just need to open the portal."

The bird waved a wing towards the wall beside the door. A round shimmering shape appeared.

"After you, Helmi bin Rashid."

Helmi walked towards the portal, stopping in front of it. He turned to Pakcik Rozaimi, a pleading look on his face.

"I will keep watch here, young Helmi. Do not worry. Should anything happen, the Orang Bunian will carry word of it to you there."

Helmi nodded. "Thanks." Then he faced the shimmering door and stepped through.

Behind him, Garuda smiled, bowed once to the old man and disappeared. The portal remained open in its wake.

# CHAPTER 13

The world Helmi stepped into was dark and gloomy. He stood on the edge of a deserted city, looking in at tall, grimy buildings with peeling paint. A hot wind blew, providing only temporary relief from the searing heat. He was sweating buckets. The longer he looked at it, the more he felt that it was vaguely familiar, like a half-forgotten dream. He blinked rapidly as the connections fell into place.

This was Kuala Lumpur sixty years ago, in the depression when money had been scarce and things had fallen into disrepair. This was the hopeless time of the city that wasn't quite yet a city, but was more than a town. He stood on its outskirts, in its extensive slums. Before the development and redevelopment projects, before the mega projects and mega buildings that would place KL on the map. Before the twin towers and the promise of a better future. This was his grandfather's and Pakcik Rozaimi's Kuala Lumpur, a place of shattered hopes and hopeful dreams. A literal city of mud.

Was this Sara's fairy land? He didn't think so. She'd talked about faded trees and little villages, about children playing games in streams and laughter that brightened the world. Why had Garuda brought him here? Where was that blasted bird anyway?

There was a streak of light and Garuda materialised.

"Sorry. Took the long way around. I don't like the portals myself," the bird apologised. "This way. You'll find that although most of the Hantu stories are told in the city, it's in the villages where they have a stronghold."

"Why is that?"

"Because the city folk have medicine and an alternate view of the world. In the villages, superstition still holds strong because they have no other beliefs to hold on to."

"I've always been in the city. My grandparents still have village minds even though they grew up here. In the city!"

"It hasn't always been a city. It started off as a village, when they were young, where they learnt all that the village had for them. But the city grew up around them and left them behind. Anyway, it's this way. We can talk while we walk."

They took a gravel road that led out from the city. Ahead of him, Helmi could see miles and miles of flat land, with some trees lining the road. They'd been walking a while before Helmi realised that it wasn't just empty land.

"What are they growing here?" he asked, staring at the neat, square plots of tilled ground. There had been no space for farm land where and when he came from.

"Rice," Garuda replied. He was flying straight in front of Helmi. The young man could tell that he was holding back his energy and his strength.

"If you need to fly ahead, just go. I'll catch up."

"It's not safe." The bird settled on Helmi's shoulder, startling him. "Keep walking."

As they walked, Helmi noted the change in scenery. Little houses started popping up along the road. They didn't seem inhabited, as far as he could tell. He asked Garuda about it.

"Spirit houses," Garuda replied. "The Hantu live in them. It's like a spiritual counterpart of the physical places in your world. They'll remain as long as those places are intact—sometimes longer—as long as people remember them."

"What about the villages we're heading towards?"

"Those are from the epics. You know all your hikayats? And those Sang Kancil stories? The people in those stories inhabit these lands."

Helmi thought about it. He knew that Sara had met Sang Kancil. But from the hikayats? "So I might actually meet Hang Tuah or Hang Jebat?"

"Why not? You've met me."

"That's true." They seemed to be walking forever. "Where's this forest we're heading to?"

"You'll see it soon."

"Isn't there some way to build this portal nearer to where we're going?"

Garuda snapped at his ear. "Be grateful for what you have. But no, the portals are linked to specific places physically, as far as we can make them work. Where Sara's apartment is is where you appeared when you went through the portal. To exit in the forest itself, you would not have been able to go through that portal. You would have had to hike up somewhere in the mountain ranges near Melawati. I did not have the time to bring you on a long hike there. This is faster."

"Isn't it the same distance though?"

"No. Because in the fairy realm, everything can be cut short. Did you not notice the speed at which the scenery has been passing you by? I have been speeding up your journey."

"Oh, so that's what it was. I thought my eyes were seeing things."

The forest now loomed in front of Helmi's eyes. He could finally understand what Sara had been saying. These forests, from afar, had seemed so real. But up close, they had this unreal quality about them. As if they were slightly transparent.

"One final question before I shut up."

"What is it?"

"Why do you think she is here in the forest and not there in the city if that is where the portal appeared?"

"Because the Hantu do not know how to use the portals, Helmi. And they have trails of their own—ones that we cannot use. As far as we can tell, they have taken her to their stronghold in the forest. Where the Lang Suir dwells. She is the strongest of them all."


Helmi could almost see the beauty of the place but he was not one of those who could dwell on his surroundings when his mind was full of worry and fear. He stumbled on, Garuda on his shoulder, into the forest, his eyes picking up on the scenery around him subconsciously; enough to keep him from stumbling and running into things, but not enough to really process what he was seeing. Which was why he missed the girl in the woods the first time. It wasn't until Garuda confronted the being that he realised that the white shape he'd been seeing was an actual spirit.

"Who are you and what do you want?" Garuda demanded again. Helmi came to a stop.

"What is that?"

"One of them."

"A Pontianak?"

"Yes. It's been following us for a while now."

"And you only speak up about it now?"

"What good would it have done you to have known about it earlier?"

"None, probably."

The creature was now beckoning to them.

"Is it wise to follow?"

"Wise? Probably not. But needs must."

Helmi set his feet towards the path that the Pontianak had shown them. Soon, they found themselves in a little village by a stream.

"Where is she? Where is Sara?" Helmi demanded.

The Pontianak merely smiled.

"Why did you bring us here?"

A Toyol came crawling out of one of the buildings. Helmi recoiled in fear and disgust.

"Helmi? Mi? Please. Help."

Helmi turned so fast he almost sprained his back. "Sa! Where are you?"

"Here!" Her voice came from another direction.

Then all around him, Sara's voice called over and over again. He looked back and forth, turning himself round and round trying to catch a glimpse of her.

"Garuda!" he called. The bird had disappeared. "Where is she?"

All he heard was the words "find her."

*But how?*

The village had filled up with a thick mist. Sara's voice still echoed in his ears. All around him, he could see the blank stares of various ghosts from his grandfather's stories. Pontianak, Toyol, Hantu Galah, Hantu Lilin, Penanggal, Hantu Tetek—whatever he'd heard of were there, surrounding him, groping at his body, even some he didn't know the names of. This wasn't a nightmare. He was in fairy land and these were real. And Sara was out there. Somewhere. He could still hear her calling him.

He brushed their hands away and closed his eyes, trying to concentrate. Amidst all the clamour that was coming from all over the place, he could hear a soft, quiet voice patiently saying *Mi. Mi. Mi.* Over and over again. He tried to fix the direction in his head and then opened his eyes to find that he was facing a small hut on the edge of the village. Ignoring everything else, he took slow, firm steps towards the hut.

Huddled in the farthest corner of the hut was Sara. She was dishevelled, still in her pyjamas, her hair covering her face. Helmi sat down beside her rocking body and put his arms around her.

The voices stopped.

"How did you know where she was?" a grating voice said.

Helmi looked up to find a lone Pontianak standing in front of them.

"Why should I tell you?"

The Pontianak shrugged. "It doesn't matter."

"What did you want with her?"

"What we all want. To be saved."

"She can't save you."

"We know that now."

"Will you leave her alone then?"

The Pontianak stared down at him, its eyes boring into his. "Why should we?"

"Because she is no use to you. What should you torture her for then?"

"Fun."

"Leave her alone."

"What will you do for us if we do? There must always be something for something, eh? A bargain?"

Helmi sighed. He knew what they wanted. There was nothing else he could do but promise. "I will write your stories for you."

"You?" It laughed, showing its pointy teeth, its black holes of eyes seeming more menacing. "You won't be half as good or half as useful as her."

"But at least you'll have something instead of nothing."

The creature nodded. "Write us. Keep us alive. Or we will haunt you forever." It disappeared into the murk outside.

"Sara?" Helmi turned back to his girlfriend. "Sa, it's safe now."

"Mi? Is that really you?"

"Yes. Yes, it is."

"How do I know? How do I know you're not another apparition?"

He tightened his arms around here. "Can't you feel me? Feel my warmth? I'm real. I'm here. Holding you."

"I... I just want to go home."

"Okay. We'll get you there. Alright?" They sat there a little longer before Helmi attempted to get up. "Come along, Sara. Let's find our way home."

# CHAPTER 14

Once Sara and Helmi exited the hut, the village seemed to fade into the background. It seemed very unreal and Helmi couldn't understand it. He couldn't understand where Garuda had disappeared to either. It was just… strange. He looked around him at the unfamiliar surroundings and wondered how to get back to the city, how long it would take for them to get there and whether the portal would even be open.

"We're going to be walking for a bit, Sara," Helmi said to her gently. "Garuda opened a portal back to your room, but we're going to have to walk a while to get to it. Are you okay with that?"

Sara nodded. "Yes. Let's just get out of here."

He tried to go back the same road they had come from. At first, it seemed to be going okay. But as they walked further, Helmi began to feel uneasy. Something didn't seem right. He hadn't really been paying attention to the scenery, but it didn't look the same to him. Nothing seemed familiar. Nothing looked like it should. He wondered if his brain was playing tricks on him. Still, he pushed on. It felt better that they were heading somewhere—even if they were heading somewhere wrong—than to keep staying in that place that was filled with bad memories.

"Did they do anything to you, Sa?" Helmi asked to fill the silence.

She didn't answer.

"Sa?" he asked, not sure if she hadn't heard the question or if they'd done something so bad to her that she couldn't talk about it.

"I… I don't know. One moment I was asleep, with you there, and then the next I was walking through the window. I fell so far, I was so afraid I'd die. It was like sitting in a roller coaster and feeling your stomach fall to the ground below you and there's nothing you can do to stop it. And there's nothing holding you to your seat. Oh! It was so frightening!"

"You walked out the window?"

"It didn't seem so much as out it as through it. I don't know if the window was actually open."

"Okay. I'm glad… I'm glad you weren't hurt."

"I was so scared I'd hit the ground and smash like a watermelon. But then I started slowing down and when I opened my eyes, I was sitting on this… something like a genie? Do you have genies? I mean, he wasn't really like an Aladdin and the genie kind of genie, but something like that."

"We have Jin, yes. And they're a little similar, but not quite."

"Okay, well, I was sitting on the Jin then. And we were flying through the air. And then we landed in that village. That was when all the creepy things I saw in my dream last night appeared again. They crowded me. Clawing at me. Pulling my clothes off. All the while they were saying, 'save us, save us,' but I didn't know how. I couldn't do a thing but curl up in a ball and cry. It was horrible, Mi. *Horrible!*"

"It's okay. You're out of it now. You're safe."

"And then I heard you calling me. But everyone else was answering in my voice. How did you know how to find me?"

Helmi smiled. "You were the only one not calling me by my name. I'm glad they didn't actually do anything to you."

"Oh, but they did!"

"You said—"

"They tore me up inside, Mi. They sucked my blood and reached into my body and tore up… they tore up my womb."

Helmi looked at her from head to toe. Other than her messy hair and wide eyes, she looked physically fine. There were no marks on her body at all.

But the tears were leaking down her face. "I'll never have children, Mi. Never."

"You don't know that, Sa. We'll get the doctor to check you over and you'll find that maybe they were lying. Maybe they were just messing with your head."

She looked at him doubtfully. "Maybe," she echoed.

"Besides, it's okay if you don't have kids. It's not my life goal or something unless you want it."

The glare on her face stopped him. Had it been her dream to have children? He didn't know. They'd never gotten round to talking about that part ever. Besides, they'd barely even been together for more than

24 hours! He didn't know how to deal with it. He sighed. And apologised.

"It's fine, Mi."

But he could see that it wasn't fine. Not knowing what to do, he concentrated instead on getting them out of the woods. That was more difficult that he thought. He had no idea where they were anymore. The road he thought had brought them seemed now to be leading them further into the forest instead of out of it. Or was it because he didn't have Garuda's power of making the road shorter than it really was? He didn't know. He was out of his depth here.

The only good part about all the walking was that Sara was starting to perk up the further they got away from that hellhole. She seemed to be taking an interest in the scenery around them, in the things that were happening, which he supposed was a good thing, seeing that he had no clue anymore where they were. He stopped walking.

"What?" she asked.

"I'm lost. I don't know where we are," he admitted.

"Oh, we're in Alam Dongeng." She gazed into the sky, something a little like peace coming over her.

He bit back most of his snark. "Which part of it?"

"The ones where the Bunians are." She turned to him suddenly. "You know, I don't know why I was so afraid of them before. They're nice. And pretty. And good."

"They kidnapped you!"

She shrugged. "I'd rather them than those others."

He nodded in agreement.


Now that Sara seemed to have her bearings, she was the one leading them. Helmi gladly let her take charge, feeling totally out of his depth. Soon, they were in a beautiful clearing with a raised dais. Beautiful fairy folk of various kinds flitted and glided around the space. They all came to a standstill, turning to watch the couple as they walked into the middle of the clearing.

"You're free!" a Bidadari approached, throwing her hands around Sara's shoulder. "Garuda said that you were under a mighty enchantment and he lost hold of Helmi in that dark, terrible place. We must tell him you're free!"

"Where is he?" Sara asked.

"He's rounding the forest calling everyone to arms. He wants to raise an army to fight the Hantu."

"Well, he can go fight them. I'd rather we beat them soundly now than they come back to attack us again," Helmi said angrily.

"Oh, but we can't do that," the Bidadari replied. "We have a pact."

"A pact? What kind of pact?"

"We keep our realms apart as much as possible. We don't like to intermingle with them. If we attack them for no reason, they will claim we have broken the pact and will come and attack us back."

"What do you mean no reason? They kidnapped and attacked Sara!"

"That would only be a valid reason if she were still in their hands, young human. Now that she is safe here, we cannot still use that ruse anymore. Otherwise, we would be just like them. Turning good into evil."

"So we can't demand for justice?"

"We can and will demand for justice," a deep male voice answered. The couple turned to see that a band of five men had entered the clearing, sharp kerises in their hands. Their leader who wore a golden headband bowed to them. "But how you demand for it is as important as that you do."

Helmi's eyes widened. "You're... are you?"

"Hang Tuah, at your service," the man replied.

"Hang Jebat."

"Hang Kesturi."

"Hang Lekir."

"Hang Lekiu."

They introduced themselves with a flourish of their hands and a deep bow at the waist. Both Helmi and Sara returned the bow.

"Is this the fair lady we were supposed to save?" Hang Kasturi asked.

"Yes, apparently her betrothed has managed to escape the enchantment with her," the Bidadari replied.

"Ah, that is good then. I am glad you are safe."

"How does it go in the world?" Hang Jebat asked.

"It... it's different," Helmi managed to say. Hang Jebat looked as if he was waiting for more, but even as Helmi tried to think of how to explain it to him, Garuda fluttered down amongst them, flustered.

"Where did you go?" Helmi asked as soon as he saw Garuda.

"Their magics booted me out. That blasted pact. I couldn't do a thing once they came at me full force. How did you get her out?"

"We... walked. I was hoping to get back to the city and the portal but we got lost. But Sara recognised the path and brought us here in hopes that one of you could help us get home."

"Walked? They let you go?"

"Once I found her, ya."

Helmi had to explain to Garuda three times what had happened before the bird decided to take him at his word. He couldn't explain the strange attack by the Hantu and he couldn't explain their strange bargain to let them go if Helmi would write about them instead.

"Nothing makes sense!" Garuda exclaimed more than once.

"I know. I've been saying that. But you're all… fairy creatures from a mythical world. Maybe nothing ever makes sense in your world."

"There must be people manipulating the story," Hang Tuah said. "Things in our world always makes sense in our world," he explained. "It's only when outside influences come to stir things up that things become strange. But don't worry, everything will resolve itself eventually."

"How do you know?" Helmi couldn't tone down the aggressiveness in his voice. He was so tired of strange things happening. Things he couldn't understand and couldn't control.

"Because this is a world of stories, Helmi. And all stories have to come to a closure, whether good or bad. And all stories have to make sense."

Helmi didn't agree with that. "Not all stories make sense."

"Because you do not see or understand that sense does not mean that somewhere, somehow it doesn't all tie in perfectly."

There was no arguing with Hang Tuah about that. Partly because Helmi didn't want to—couldn't—argue with a personal hero of his, but also because he didn't understand the issues deeply enough. If he had been swimming in deep waters before, he was now in the middle of the sea without even a sampan to keep him afloat.

"I think we should go home now," he finally said. Garuda agreed.

"Do we need to walk back to that city place, or can you just open a portal here for us to go home?"

"If we open the portal here, you'll end up in the mountains."

Helmi sighed. It looked like they had a lot more walking to do.

# CHAPTER 15

Walking with Sara turned out to be more agreeable than walking with Garuda alone. For one, he enjoyed her company a lot more and for another, now that she wasn't in shock, she was telling him little tidbits about the fairy world—both Alam Dongeng and the Old Fairy Kingdom—to entertain him.

"So the house actually has legs? And walks?" he asked in surprise when she told him about Baba Yaga's hut.

"Yes. Have you never heard of her before?"

He shook his head.

"It's an old tale from Russia. There are many versions of them. But the Baba Yaga I saw the other day was a rather kind old woman. She reminded me of my grandmother."

"In what way?"

"Oh, I don't know. It's not like a physical similarity. Obviously, she's Russian and my grandmother is totally Chinese. But I suppose it's this look they have—like they have the ability to see into your soul and read it. And tell you that you've been a silly girl, but it's going to be alright."

"That's nice." Helmi couldn't remember much of his grandmother. She'd died when he was ten. They had never been particularly close. She had been sick for most of those ten years, and when she had finally died, he'd felt an awful sense of relief. He hadn't told anyone though. It still made him feel a little guilty twenty years on.

"She did seem to think that I'd be able to do something. Or had done something. I'm not sure which anymore."

It struck Helmi as funny how everyone seemed to be pinning their hopes on Sara. It wasn't a ha-ha, how funny kind of funny, but more of a that's-odd, why's-that kind of funny. Did he feel a little jealous of the attention? Earlier on no, but now that he was here, maybe a little. He tried to push aside the feeling. These creatures were threatening his girlfriend, for goodness' sake. The vagaries of human nature, he supposed. But he was tired of circling around the issue. Whether she could and would help them was one thing. For him, the most important thing was getting them off his—and her—backs, so that they could go back to life as usual. A new life as usual.

They'd reached the desolate city and Sara was decrying the despondency and the disrepair.

"We should go, Sara," he said, trying to distract her from it.

Garuda agreed with him, directing them to where the portal was still shimmering in place. Funny; he hadn't noticed it until Garuda had mentioned it. Was it not meant for him to see? Maybe.

Sara didn't want to go first, so they stepped through together. Helmi felt relieved when the familiar walls of Sara's apartment came into view. Rozaimi was sitting on the couch, looking up as soon as he saw the movement. A look of relief spread across his face. Helmi wondered briefly where his grandfather was, when the door to Sara's room opened and Abdul Mansoor came out of it, rubbing his face wearily.

"Sara, I think you should leave this house," he said, not bothering with cordiality.

"What? Why?"

"It's not safe for you here at this moment."

"I can't just leave and find a new place in a day," Sara snapped back.

Helmi was about to snarl a retort, but Abdul Mansoor stilled him with a wave of his hand. "Come stay with us. It will be safer there."

"What?" Helmi exclaimed.

Abdul Mansoor ignored his grandson. "What if they come after you again? The Hantu now know how to find you. If you stay here, no one can protect you. If you come with us, I will be able to help."

Sara exhaled loudly. Helmi stood beside her, confusion clear on his face. How would his grandfather be able to help? Why would he want Sara to stay with them? What was the old man trying to do?

"Adik, I know you don't like it. But safety should come first," Pakcik Rozaimi chimed in. "Apa salahnya? You'll be staying with people who would care for you properly."

She caved. "Fine. I'll go pack my things."

Helmi watched Sara head to her bedroom. His grandfather watched her receding back with a strange look in his eyes.

"Atuk? What's going on?"

Abdul Mansoor pressed his lips tight. "I don't like the feel of this place."

Sara's scream pierced through the room.

At first sight the bedroom seemed to be filled with a mountain of flesh. Helmi pushed his way in front of Sara, hoping to shield her from whatever it was. Two large eyes peered out at him. They backed out of the room, bumping into Rozaimi and Abdul Mansoor.

"Ya Allah, it's the Gedembai!" Rozaimi exclaimed. Abdul Mansoor's eyes narrowed but he stayed silent.

"What's that?" Helmi asked. "You mean it's not just a giant?"

"No—it's like a Gergasi, a giant, but it can turn you to stone."

"What's it doing in my room?" Sara's voice rose in pitch, as if she couldn't control it anymore. Helmi could feel her shaking behind him. It was too much. Too much for one day.

"Get out of there, you foul beast!" he screamed at it, feeling very much not like a knight in shining armour. "*Keluar, raksasa!*" he added for good measure, just in case it didn't understand English.

There was a rumbling, grumbling sound from inside the room. Helmi realised it was the Gedembai speaking. "I do not mean to harm you," it was saying in slow, archaic Malay. "I stumbled here by accident and I cannot find my way home."

"Why is my house a seismic pothole of portals to the fairy kingdom?" Sara wailed when Helmi translated it for her. She was too shaken and too bewildered to figure out anything else anymore.

"The portal here was opened by Garuda. The one in your room must have been opened by the Hantu. Only they forgot to close it," Rozaimi surmised. "But how come we did not see it?"

"It was *closed*," Abdul Mansoor hissed under his breath.

Helmi turned to look at him briefly in puzzlement. "I couldn't really see the one Garuda opened until he pointed it out. Maybe this one works that way too? That could be why the Gedembai stumbled into it."

"I don't care, Mi. I don't want to live here anymore!" Sara crumpled on the couch in sobs.

"Just hold on a little longer, Sa. I'll get your things from the room and we can go."

Rozaimi nodded. "You go ahead. Let us figure out how to deal with this."

"Where's the spare key, Sa? We should leave one with them and take one with us."

Sara nodded, pointing to the cupboard above the kitchen sink. "In the empty Milo tin."

She sat on the couch, Abdul Mansoor beside her whilst Helmi went to retrieve the keys. He passed them to Rozaimi and then went into Sara's room, mumbling under his breath to the giant. The giant rumbled something back and then fell quiet.

"What do you need, Sara?" Helmi called from the room. He figured he'd grab the basics, but he didn't know if there was anything else that she might want.

"Anything. Clothes."

Minutes later, Helmi reappeared with her luggage bag. "Uh, I basically stuffed almost everything I could find in here. I don't really know what you want. But everything should be there. Oh wait." He disappeared for a while and she could hear some clinking. "I remembered your toothbrush."

Before they left, Abdul Mansoor pulled Helmi to the side.

"I'll do what I can here, but please, keep her away from this place. It is now riddled with too many openings to the enchanted world, and with the number of creatures—both good and bad—who are trying to find her, I do not think it safe for her to be here anymore. I am glad the Toyol has not adopted her, but you do not know what kinds of creatures may come after her, some of which may be worse than an unadopted Toyol."

Helmi nodded. He took Sara by the elbow. They walked out of the house without looking back.

# CADENCE

He shuts himself into Sara's room. There's no point in involving the others—Helmi is too worried and Rozaimi can't see them. Let Garuda distract them with plans of extraction.

"Do you see me?" he asks.

It is silent for a long while. He begins to think he is mistaken when they suddenly appear. They're no taller than six, maybe seven centimetres, looking up at him with worry written on their faces. They're furry, despite their human-like appearance. Part of his mind calls them little grey monkeys. It's not like he hasn't seen their like before, in a different time, a different place. It's a family, he realises. Grandfather, mother, five children. Where is the father?

"What have you seen?" he asks the grandfather. The older Kenit turns to the woman. He's surprised. Matriarchal? Unusual in these parts.

"The Lang Suir herself opened the portal," the mother says, pointing at the window. "But the Raja was with her."

He frowns, walking towards the window, pushing it open. He tilts his head, looking out at an angle with squinted eyes, searching. Ah, there it is. He can see it now, the little slit where the portal is closed. His searching fingers feel the pulse of magic, but he can't open it. Can't manipulate it.

A hiss of power leaks through. *Pengkhianat.*

He shivers. "I never betrayed him," he says half to himself, half to the Orang Kenit clustered around his feet, though he can't say why.

"Is it true?"

He looks at the one who spoke. The grandfather. The only one who might have known of him. Might have known him then. He peers closer but doesn't recognise the face. "I am he."

The mother looks confused.

It's the grandfather who answers, "Putera Abdul Mansoor, Raja Bunian's changeling son."

"Exiled son," Abdul Mansoor murmurs absently, wondering what to do next.

# CHAPTER 16

Mary could not sleep. She'd lain awake in bed for a long time, thinking a little about her life, but quite a lot about Sara. She hadn't really expected the girl to contact her—it was a long shot at any rate, asking the girl to look her up on the Internet; she was hardly famous—but for some reason, she was a little worried. Well, lying in bed staring at the ceiling was not going to help her. She was old enough that she didn't care about lack of sleep. She could fall asleep easily any time in the day anyway, so it wasn't as if she couldn't catch up on it. If anything, she should be worried about sleeping too much. She decided to go for a walk. It was not too late to slip into the Old Fairy Kingdom before the portal closed.

There was a bit of frost touching the leaves. Mary pulled her sweater close, bracing herself against the cold wind. Ataneq's cottage was dark.

"Just like him to be asleep at this time," she muttered to herself. She went deeper into the kingdom. The night creatures were out and about, most of them giving her a wide berth both for the human scent as well as her bloodline to the Queen. She wanted to head to the Malaysian forest but she didn't want to go alone. Who else could she persuade to go with her? She stopped by Euthalia's tree, but the dryad was nowhere to be seen.

"Probably sleeping too," Mary murmured to herself. Eventually, she found Charon with his wife, Sophea, stargazing in the fields.

"What are you doing about so late at night, Mary?" Charon asked.

"I couldn't sleep so I decided to go for a walk."

"It's a nice clear night for a walk," Charon agreed. "But you don't look like that's all you've set out to do."

"That girl who came by the other day. Remember her? We introduced her to the Centaur Council."

Charon nodded. "What about her?"

"I don't think things are going well with her."

"How would you know? Has she sent you a message of any kind?"

Mary shook her head. "No, nothing of the sort. It's just a vague feeling."

Charon raised an eyebrow. "And?"

"I'm a little worried, Charon," Mary admitted. "Would you mind if you and Sophea accompanied me on a walk?"

"Where to?"

"To that new annexe. I want to see if there's been anything strange going on."

"I do think you're worried about nothing," Charon replied. "But we'll go with you. I do have a curiosity about that place. It's not every day that a new world appears."

Mary smiled. She'd grown much taller since the time she had first seen Charon, but she was still way shorter than any of the centaurs. They walked amicably together, Mary making a little valley between the two of them.

"What else is new with you?" Sophea asked.

Mary nattered about her family. Jane's granddaughter had just given birth to a baby girl so she was a great-grandaunt now. It made her feel old and she said so.

Charon laughed. "You're only up to one great. We have probably five or six greats appended to our titles!"

"It's different for you when you don't grow old, Charon. You don't feel the aches and the pains that I do. Sometimes I feel like just giving up and dying."

"Don't say that, Mary," he admonished.

"It's the truth. I won't do it, of course, but I won't say that I'm adverse to just lying down and never getting up again."

"You'll feel different when Elizabeth comes to visit and puts the new baby in your arms. What's her name anyway?"

"Bernice," Mary replied. "Bernice Mary. Doesn't that sound nice?"

"It does indeed. Especially since she's named after you."

There was a rustling in the brush. The sky was bright now and the air was warm. Mary took off her sweater. Charon lifted his head and sniffed. There had been too much rustling, unlike the Old Fairy Kingdom. Were the creatures really that bad at hiding, or were they intentionally trying to signal their presence?

"What's wrong?" Mary asked.

"Nothing. It just smells different." He sneezed. "Whatever you are, why don't you just come out?" Charon said. "We can smell you, you know."

Several tiny, human like beings stepped into view.

"Who are you?" Charon asked.

"We are Orang Kenit," their spokesperson said in accented English.

"Dwarves? Imps?" Mary asked.

They shook their heads collectively. There was a brief, hurried discussion, but none of them could come to a consensus on the correct translation.

"It doesn't matter," the Kenit spokesperson finally said. "We are what we are."

"Were you following us?" Charon asked.

"We crossed your path a short way back."

"Why?"

Another brief discussion.

"I don't trust them," Mary whispered to Charon.

"There is war brewing on the horizon," their spokesperson finally said. "We would like to know whose side you are on."

"Side? We're not on anyone's side." Charon harrumphed. "We are of the Old Fairy Kingdom. We do not involve ourselves in your petty wars."

"All very nice and well to say, Charon dear, but we are in their territory," his wife muttered.

More muted conversation.

"But you are of the Penglipur Lara's kind, yes?" the spokesperson spoke directly to Mary.

"Me? What's this Lara thing?"

"Our... Storyteller. You are of her kind? Her species?"

"You mean Sara? Well, yes. I am human. Mostly."

"Then you must bear witness."

"To what?"

"To what must come."

With those ominous words, the small humanoids disappeared in a cloud of smoke.

"What... what was that about?" Mary said, somewhat shaken.

Charon shook his head. "I don't understand it. What war is happening? Why should we—or even you—be involved?"

"I told you I had a bad feeling about this."

"Well, yes. Now I have a bad feeling too. And it wasn't the grass we ate this evening."

Mary rolled her eyes.

They continued walking, various worried expressions on their faces. Mary was glad she'd listened to her instincts. It seemed that things were afoot in Alam Dongeng, things that only were revealed at night. Strange. Nights were for sleeping. Not for plotting. But perhaps they did things differently in far parts of the world—then again, it *was* morning in those far parts of the world.

It wasn't long before they found themselves in the Orang Bunian's territory. The place looked like it was just beginning to wake up, filled with frenetic bustle pushing against sluggish activity. It was with some difficulty that they found the Raja and Permaisuri Bunian.

"War? Yes, there is war coming," Permaisuri Bunian said when pressed. "I don't know if it will involve you, but yes, it does involve the Penglipur Lara."

"But why?" Mary pressed.

"Both sides want her, of course. Ours, because we found her, and because she has a beautiful way with us. Theirs because... I don't know. They have always wanted to take what is ours. They have always wanted to corrupt us—and corrupt the humans—with their lust for power and greed."

The Raja, his facility with language not as good as his wife's, nodded. "*Derhaka.*"

"What's that?" Charon asked.

"Sin," Permaisuri Bunian said curtly.

"How can we help?" Mary said.

That caused the royal couple to pause. "Why would you want to help?"

"Because I care about Sara. After all, she is my kind, as you seem to like to put it. I care what happens to her. And she's young. She has a life ahead of her. I'd like her to see that life if I can."

"Then convince her to help us, Mary Hays, daughter of Queens. She has power but she does not use it. She must."

"How is she able to help you?"

"By telling our stories."

So it was that old thing again. Did it never end? Was this cycle always to perpetuate?

"If she will change them, they would not attack her. They would have no cause to do so, do you see? She could change them for good.

Change them so that this war would not happen," the Permaisuri said eagerly.

That struck Mary as odd. "Why change only them? Why not change you as well?"

"But we are not the ones thirsting for blood. All we want is to live in peace."

So they were using Sara, after all. Using her for their own gain despite all their cries for help. "And what would this peace look like?"

"The Orang Halus living in peace, with us as their leaders. We would govern them well. The Hantu would be banished forever, never to haunt us or humans again. They would not be given the freedom to roam and hurt people."

"Why do you think they hurt people?"

"Why do we care? It is a fact that they do and it cannot be tolerated any longer!"

Mary came to a decision. "I will talk to Sara, Your Majesties. How can I get in contact with her?"

"We will bring her to you."

Mary shook her head. "No, I would rather go to her. Is that possible?"

There was a brief, heated discussion.

"This way," Permaisuri Bunian finally said.

The Raja and Permaisuri Bunian led Mary, Charon and Sophea down a long path. They soon left the forest far behind and passed by cultivated farmlands.

"Where are you taking us?" Charon asked eventually.

"The only portal we know," the Permaisuri said. "It leads you directly to Sara's house in the city. So it opens in the city as well."

"Do you not have any portals in the forest?"

"We know of one other," the Permaisuri said, "but it is far from where you wish to go. I would not know if anyone would be able to lead you from that portal to where the Penglipur Lara is."

"What does that term mean anyway?" Mary asked.

"It is like a story teller. A bard. But in truth, it means the reliever of sorrows. Traditionally the Penglipur Lara tells you stories to take away the burdens of the day."

"That sounds nice."

"Is it still far from here?" Charon asked again.

"No, it is a short distance away. We will be reaching soon."

Charon nodded. "What is it that you plan to do, Mary?"

"I will go through the portal, of course."

"How will you get back?"

"Through this same portal, I'm supposing."

"You're leaving a lot to chance, aren't you?" Charon said.

"Haven't I always?"

The three old friends shared a smile.

"But what will you do there?" Charon pressed.

Mary shrugged. "I really do not have any idea. But Sara needs guidance and if I am to take my role as a protector of the Old Fairy Kingdom seriously, then this is the task that is set before me."

Their guides came to a stop slightly before the edge of the city.

"This portal leads you into Sara's home. Do not ask us why it does, for we do not know either. We will post sentries around this portal to look out for your return."

Mary thanked them and turned to the centaurs. "Oh, do a favour for me, will you? Could you get someone to let Jane and Ataneq know where I am? I don't want them to worry. Maybe someone should keep a watch on my house too."

Charon smiled and clasped her hand. "Don't worry, Mary. All will be well."

"Come back to us soon. And safely," his wife said.

Mary waved and stepped through the portal.

# CHAPTER 17

Mary found herself in an extremely crowded apartment. First of all, there was a giant in the bedroom bellowing to be set free. Then there were dozens of Bunians milling about uselessly. And then there was another set of Kenits that seemed to be having a full blown argument right in the living room. Finally, there was a very old man sitting at the dining table, massaging his temples. No, she corrected herself, there was a second old man staring at her from beneath beetled brows, standing by the doorway, as if trying to decide what to do.

He stepped nearer to her, arm raised. She stumbled backwards, wondering if he was threatening her. He sighed, seeming to come to a decision. "Abdul Mansoor." His hand shifted direction.

She took it hesitantly. "Mary Hays."

"Who sent you here?"

"I… I was looking for Sara."

Abdul Mansoor's lips quirked upwards. "Sara? No, but who *sent* you here? How did you find this portal?"

"The… Bunians showed me." She could see the other Bunians in the room gesturing frantically at her. To keep quiet? To keep them secret?

"Ah." Abdul Mansoor's inflection was flat. She wondered what that was about. "No matter. Can *you* open portals?"

"Me? How do I do that?"

"You came through one. I would have to expect that you have some form of magical affinity?"

"Yes. It comes with the family. My grandmother is the Fairy Queen. My grandfather is the King of the Elves." She wasn't sure why she felt the need to explain.

"Good. Then you can help me." Abdul Mansoor walked into the bedroom, laying a calming hand on the Gedembai. "Hush, we will get you out soon."

The Gedembai stilled, watching them with narrowed eyes.

"We can't get her out of here through the door. So we need to get her out through the portal she came through." He gestured at the open window. "The problem is that my magic has been sealed. I cannot open the portal, even though I know it is there."

"Sealed?" Mary asked, cocking her head to the right. She stepped to the window, peering outside. It took her a while to find it. "It's closed."

"Exactly. I need you to open it."

"How do I do that?" She'd never opened a closed portal before. The ones she knew were magically spelled to open and close by her grandmother.

Abdul Mansoor gave her a few instructions and she repeated them. The portal opened, shining bright through the window. He nodded and turned, speaking to the Gedembai softly, the words rolling off his tongue in measured cadences. Measured. Calming. Strong.

The Gedembai seemed to calm as she listened, and then it glanced suspiciously at the window. Abdul Mansoor continued to talk, coaxing until it slowly turned, crawling in the narrow space to the portal.

Mary sighed when it disappeared from sight, leaving a quiet, if messy, room.

"It wasn't a coincidence," Abdul Mansoor said, still staring out the window.

"What do you mean?"

"The portal was closed earlier. I'm sure of that. I left the room. Talked to Sara and Helmi. She entered the room to pack her things and found the Gedembai here. I sent them both away, but when I came back in to check, the portal was still closed. A scare tactic?"

"Whose side is it on?"

Abdul Mansoor jerked. "What?"

"Is it a good or bad creature?"

"It is what it is. Neither good nor bad."

"No, no, that's not what I mean." Mary was staring at the open portal. She closed it, not wanting anything else to come into the room. "Is it on the Bunian's side or the other side?"

He mulled the question. "If I had to say, it would be one of the Orang Bunian's followers."

"And you?"

His mouth set itself into a thin, grim line. He didn't answer her.

When they left the room, Mary found that the Bunians had disappeared.

"I sent them away," the man in the room said. "Oh, who are you?"

Abdul Mansoor introduced them to each other, before lifting an eyebrow and asking, "Sent who away?"

"The Bunians," Rozaimi answered.

"They were… did they say anything?" Abdul Mansoor asked. Mary wondered at the whisper of longing in his voice.

Rozaimi shook his head.

Mary frowned. "You cannot see them? But you could see the giant?"

"I could see the Gedembai, yes. I can see most of the creatures of legend. But Aria has blocked me from seeing or hearing any of his people," Abdul Mansoor said.

She bit at her lower lip as she thought about that. "And sealed your magic."

She thought that he stiffened a little before saying, "Yes, that too."

"And what of these little people here? The, ah, Orang Kenit, I think they said?"

"I see them. I have spoken to them."

Rozaimi looked confused. "There are Orang Kenit here?"

"Why is it that you can see and hear the Bunian but not these?" Mary asked.

Rozaimi scratched at his neck. "Ah, it depends on your powers, miss. I have been granted the powers to see some kinds of Orang Halus, but not all."

"Orang Halus?"

"The fine… fine people. It is what we call them—all of them."

"Like a general term? The way I say the fairy folk?"

"Yes, yes. That's it."

"The important question now, I suppose, is what they're doing here?"

Abdul Mansoor gave her a confused look. "Why shouldn't they be here?"

"It's normal? Shouldn't there be an agreement of some kind? I can't feel any."

The two men exchanged glances, before Abdul Mansoor finally said, "The permission is… implied? If the house owner did not want them here, they would not be allowed to stay."

"Many people often bless the houses before they move in," Rozaimi explained when Mary looked even more confused. "It doesn't matter which religion. The Christians, the Muslims, the Hindus—well, maybe except the Buddhists—all pray that whichever god they believe in will bless the house and chase away the spirits. Though we all know that the only true God is Allah."

"So, they were effectively prayed away," she said hesitantly.

Rozaimi nodded.

"And Sara did not do that here."

There was a short discussion between Abdul Mansoor and the Kenit, before he nodded. "No, she did not. She seemed unaware of their presence and they did what they could to keep it that way. They have been here for five years."

Mary yawned as she nodded. She had really been up all night and she was tired. She glanced at the clock and realised that it was almost twelve. She stared at it for a moment, confused. Hadn't she left home at midnight? How could that be? She'd been running around and doing so many things, but it definitely hadn't taken twenty-four hours. Then she looked out the window and realised that it was noon, not midnight.

"I'm going to take a nap. Will… will Sara be back soon?"

Abdul Mansoor shook his head. "Sara was planning to stay over at my son's house until all this is over."

"Oh. Will you take me to her then? After all, I came here to talk to her."

"I will arrange something."

Mary nodded, laid down on the couch and went to sleep.

# SEQUENCE

*And you?*

Her question rings in his head, hours after she asked it.

Whose side is he on? Whose side *should* he be on? Aria has disowned, exiled him. The Lang Suir wants his help. Baba Yaga wants to use him as a sword. Sara and Helmi want his stories, his words. He is pinned down by expectations, by needs on all sides.

*And you?*

He wants to go home. It isn't his home. He doesn't want to go. He can't. But he needs to. He wants… He doesn't know what he wants. Everything is falling apart and it's all his fault. It's not his fault. It's Aria's. It's no one's. It's death and decay, life and rebirth, it's the cycle of time spinning, spinning, and what he once thought was immortal is now feeling the pang of death. No, not the pang of death—the claws of change. Still—

*And you?*

Abdul Mansoor feels a volcano of emotions erupting. Festering anger at what Aria and Nur have done, at duplicity, at betrayal, at *murder*. Bristling pride claws to regain all that he has lost, what was stolen, what was *taken*. Howling pain pierces his heart, spears his soul. Chilling fear slips down his spine: going back means death. He is sure of it.

Barely scabbed wounds, though it had all been so long ago. Everything is still so fresh. Raw. He is a creature of the ages, has been for as long as he can remember, even though his time is coming soon.

*And you?*

"I am on *my* side."

# CHAPTER 18

"Here? What do you mean she's here?" Helmi scratched his chin as he stood by the doorway to his office.

"She came out of the portal. A white woman. Mary, like she said." Abdul Mansoor made an impatient noise.

"She's sleeping at Sara's apartment now?"

"Yes."

"Are you still there?"

"Tak lah. Once the Gedembai left, we left too."

"So she's there alone."

"Yes, I already said that."

"Okay, okay. I'll talk to Sara and see if she's okay with going over for a while later."

"I left your number with her, but I realised that Sara's house doesn't have a house phone."

"Yeah. Well. We'll work something out. Thanks, Atuk."

"Helmi. The Kenit have been living with Sara for the past five years. Maybe we should do a cleansing."

"She's not Muslim, 'tuk. I don't know if she will agree to that. Anyway, I need to go now. I will talk to Sara and update you later."

"Okay. Bye."

Helmi hung up and stood there a little longer, staring into space. He pinged Sara's office communicator and asked her to come over.

"What's up?" She stood beside him, wiping her hands on a paper towel.

"We have a new problem."

She froze. "What?" Her voice dropped to a frightened whisper.

"Well, the good news is that the Gedembai is out of your bedroom. The bad news is that there is a portal in your bedroom, which is how it got in. The other bad news is… Aunty Mary has come to visit."

"Aunty Mary?" Her face crinkled in confusion. "How did Aunty Mary get here?"

"Apparently, she walked into the Old Fairy Kingdom on her end, crossed into Alam Dongeng and then stepped through the portal… into your house." He let that sink in for a while and then asked as gently as he could, "Do you want to see her? At your place?"

Her yes was decisive.

"Okay then. We'll go after work."

Mary was rummaging through the fridge when Helmi and Sara came in.

"Oh, hello," she greeted them, popping her head over the fridge door. "I was just getting hungry. I don't know what all these things are and if I can eat them?"

Sara went over to look. Most of them were the leftovers from dinner the other day. "Sure, they should be fine." She popped the container into the microwave. "Oh Aunty Mary, I'm so glad you're here. I've been having such a horrible time." The old woman listened sombrely to Sara's tale, nodding at frequent intervals.

"But why are you here?" she asked at the end.

The old woman smiled. "I was worried about you. But more than that—I came here to tell you about the war."

"The war?" Helmi's interest perked. He'd only been half-listening earlier, but now he turned his full attention on Mary.

"I don't know all the details," she disclaimed, "but this is what I've gathered from my conversation with the Raja and Permaisuri of the Orang Bunian. The Orang Halus and the Hantu have been at war for centuries. They're fighting for supremacy in their land. I gather that the Hantu have been winning—something to do with the affinity of your people for horror stories? I'm not sure if I understood that right—and so the Halus have been trying to find something that will gain them the upper hand. That something is apparently you."

"Me? Why me?" Sara felt that she'd been asking that question too many times over the course of the past few weeks, but there it was again.

"They're trying to use you for their own ends. They believe, rightly or wrongly, that if you 'change' the Hantu into nicer, better legends, they will win the war. The Hantu will lose their haunting power and will become subject to them."

"So, it's not just about their land which is fading?"

"Well, it is fading, that's for sure, but I gather that's not their main concern. They're just using that to get you on their side."

"And what do the Hantu believe?" Helmi asked.

"I don't know. I haven't talked to them."

Sara laid out the various containers of heated up food on the table. "Go ahead and eat," she said.

"Aren't you eating too?" Mary asked.

"Oh no, we're going back to Helmi's place for dinner. His mother's already cooked."

"Great. I'll tuck in then."

There was a momentary silence as Mary started to eat.

"So what do we do?" Sara finally asked.

"That's totally up to you, Sara. You're the Storyteller. You get to decide."

"But I don't know how my words are going to affect anything!"

"None of us know either, Sara. This is totally new ground to me. My fight was to get the stories told in the first place. Nobody cared whether it was right or wrong, whether it fit canon or changed it. It was simpler, back in my day. I don't envy you this. I just wanted to make sure that whatever you do, you're doing it because you want to. You're not being badgered or frightened or bullied into it. And I wanted you to go in knowing what you're facing. I don't like the fact that they're trying to manipulate you. Both sides. It's not right.

"Another thing, Sara. I don't know what this big deal is about you writing about them. I don't think it can be that different from our fairy world, but you don't have to write about them. You don't have to change the stories. All you have to do is learn them. Love them. They write themselves. I've never written a darned thing in my whole life. All I've done is shared my love for the stories with my friends. With my family. With children. Don't take all of this on yourself because your fairy creatures are selfish and want to push you into doing things. They're bullies, if you ask me. Big fat bullies." She emphasised the last three words with three jabs of her finger.

"Thank you."

"One other thing. You really have to get control of your house imps."

"What?"

"Didn't either of those men tell you? Your place is infested with them. The Kenit things. They're running riot everywhere!"

"I… I never knew," she stammered. "I don't see anything."

"Haven't you noticed things moving around? Things going missing? Stuff like that?"

Sara blushed. "I always just assumed that I was being careless. It's not as if I'm a very neat person."

"Well, I don't doubt that, but it's not entirely new. The only good thing about them is that I've been able to bully them into cleaning up the mess the Gedembai made of your bedroom."

"How did you manage to do that?" Helmi asked.

"Sign language, mostly. I don't understand a word they say, and they don't seem to understand me—or at least they don't admit that they do, but the power of a witch is very useful even without words." Mary smiled beatifically.

Sara and Helmi stared at her.

"Didn't I tell you my grandmother is the Fairy Queen?"

Sara nodded whilst Helmi shook his head.

"Well, it's not just in theory." She finished eating, snapped her fingers and pointed to the plates and then to the sink. Helmi and Sara watched in amazement as the plates seemed to walk themselves to the sink and wash up.

"How did you—" Sara was flabbergasted.

"I wrote down some words for you. It's in English, of course, but they should work fine when you translate them to Malay. And they will work for you because you are the owner of this house."

"Uh, I rent it."

"Well, the person who lives in this house then."

"But I can't even see them!"

"I don't know why you would want to, but once you say these words and get them under your power, you will be able to see and hear them." She leaned forward and whispered conspiratorially. "They're really noisy creatures."

"Will it work for me?" Helmi asked.

Mary looked a little uncertain. "I don't know. I've never tried it that way. The imps at home listen to my mother and to me. But I've never had my father try it."

"How do you know it will work for me? I don't have any magical blood like you," Sara asked.

"House imps work for the primary inhabitants of the house. I don't see why it shouldn't work the same way just because they're slightly different from what we have at home."

"Thanks, I think. I'll… I'll probably try it out later. I don't know if I can bear to see any other spirit thing at this point of time."

"No worries, dear. I understand how you feel. It's been a trying time for you." She rose to her feet. "Well, I've spoken to you and I've given you all the help I think I can. And I have your phone number now. Let me give you mine. If anything happens, give me a call or a text or something and I will pop over as soon as my tired old legs will let me!"

She scribbled down her number for Sara.

"I really had better get home. I'm sure there are people there who would be worrying about me by now. Toodle-doo!"

With a wave of her hand, she walked into the wall and disappeared.

Sara and Helmi sat for a while, looking at each other in subdued shock.

"Time to go back?" Helmi said a few minutes later.

"I suppose so."

They cleared up and locked up the apartment then left for Helmi's home.

# CHAPTER 19

That night, on the floor of the spare room Dina had put her in, Sara laid out sheets and sheets of paper. On each one, she wrote the name of each fairy creature she had met or heard of. Once she was done, she started to pen in all the details she could remember of each of them. It took her quite a while, and her back ached once she was done. She stretched out on the bed for a while to ease the pain. There was a knock on the door.

"Who is it?"

"Me."

"Come in! It's open."

Helmi opened the door and stepped in. He stopped, looking at the papers on the floor and tiptoed gingerly around them to get in far enough to close the door.

"What's all this?" he asked.

"Just starting preliminaries," she said, propping her head up on her arm to look at him.

"We do have tables, you know."

"I know. I just… needed more space."

"You're one weird woman."

"I know. That's why you like me." She grinned teasingly at him for a few seconds before the smile dropped from her face.

"What's wrong?" he asked.

"Nothing. I'm just so tired. So, so tired. And I don't know where to start."

"Start with what you know."

"That's the problem, Helmi! I know nothing! Look at what I've come up with. Name: Orang Bunian. Description: Reminds me of elves. Tall.

Graceful. Beautiful. Can enchant you. And that's it! And they are the ones I've talked to the most! How is this going to help anyone or anything?"

"Well, then write anything you can think of. It's their problem then, isn't it? They're only getting what they asked for."

"I suppose," she said, pouting.

"Let's do this."

"Let's?"

"I bargained to do it for the Hantu didn't I? I'd better keep to my word. So now tell me everything you know about writing a story."

"Everything?" Sara laughed. "That's going to take a long time."

"So you better get started."

"No closed doors in my house, the two of you!" a yell came from downstairs.

Helmi rolled his eyes. "What does she think we're doing? We're not teens anymore, for crying out loud."

There was a banging on the door. It flew open.

Helmi turned to face his mother, his hands up. "What?"

"Just checking," she said with a twinkle in her eye. "I won't have it said that there were goings-on in my house under my watch."

"Okay, okay. Let's head down to the dining room," Helmi said, turning to Sara. "That's probably big enough to hold all your papers."

Sara nodded, pushing herself off the bed. Dina nodded and walked away, leaving the door wide open.

"That's another thing we should be talking about, Mi."

"What? My mother chaperoning us?"

"No, I mean, our relationship. At work. I don't know if it's a good idea seeing that I'm... well, reporting directly to you."

Helmi sighed. "You're right. I was thinking about that earlier today, but I didn't want to bring it up." He bent and started picking up the papers, shuffling them into a neat pile.

"What does that mean?" Did that mean he wanted to break up? Sara gulped. This was going to be the shortest relationship in the history of the world.

"I'm going to have to self-report this to management. See what they say. They'll probably swap our departments or something, you know. So that you report to someone else. Or shift branches."

"That's fair enough."

"I know it is. But it means I won't be there to protect you."

"From what?"

"All these... crazy supernatural things!"

"I'm sure… I'm sure I'll be fine. They can't touch me at work, can they? And there will be people all around. All you have to do is make sure you're there during the befores and afters."

He still looked a little glum, but nodded in agreement.

"Well, we'll see. It's… it's going to be a change, isn't it?"

"All life is change," she quoted with a laugh. "Come on, I have a long lecture to give you on writing stories."

They headed down to the dining room.

Two hours later, Sara stood up and tore the paper to shreds.

"It's not going to work, Helmi. I don't know enough. I feel like I'm messing things up. I'm putting them in places and situations that are all wrong. It's all wrong, Mi. I don't like it."

He looked up from his own paper. "I'm still on my first sentence. Don't look at me like that."

"I can't do this, Mi. I've said it before and I'll say it again. I can't. And I won't."

"Fine. Don't. We'll just head back to your house, pop into fairy land and tell them no."

"I can't do that, Mi!" she wailed.

"Then what? You can't write and you can't tell them you can't write. What then?"

"Urgh, I don't know." She sunk back onto the chair despondently.

Her handphone beeped. She reached over, checked her messages and gasped. Helmi looked up.

"What?"

"I've destroyed it. I've destroyed Alam Dongeng."

"How?"

"Read it yourself." She thrust the phone at him. He took it and scanned through the message from Mary.

"I told you. I told you I didn't know enough! I told you I didn't know what I was doing!"

"No, you shouldn't blame yourself for this. They were the ones who were trying to pressure you into it. I guess their plan backfired."

"How do I fix this?"

"Who says you have to?"

"I have to fix this."

"And I say you don't."

They glared at each other over the table.

"Look, it's not your fault, Sara. You need to calm down."

"Maybe we should go over and see what happened."

Helmi nodded. "Yes, but not tonight."

"But—"

"It's late, Sa. You're tired. You're upset. Tonight, you go to sleep and tomorrow morning, when you are fresh, we can go over and see what's happening. Deal?"

"Early morning?"

"Yes. Early morning. Deal?" He stuck out his hand.

She wavered a little before she took it. "Deal."

"Now go get some rest."

Reluctantly, she went back up the stairs and headed to her room. She texted Mary back to let her know their plans, switched off the lights and tried to get some sleep.

# DISSONANCE

The world is changing. She is sure of it.

She opens her eyes and looks at the ceiling. The design on the plaster cast stands out in stark relief, sharper than she has ever seen them. If she had ever seen them. Her half-frown smooths out, memories of intricately-weaved attap leaves momentarily forgotten. The house is warming up in the sun. Its whiteness glares in her eyes; she makes a mental note to repaint them in a more inviting colour. She blinks once, remembering bare, shabby wooden walls with holes that let in air and rain. The image fades quickly.

She slips her feet into the soft bedroom slippers that wait beside her four-poster bed and goes down to the kitchen for a cup of water. For a moment, she wonders when her house had grown taller but sunk lower. It used to be that she climbed the ramshackle stairs to get into her house on stilts, instead of going down marble stairs from her bedroom to the kitchen. The world is changing. What is it changing into?

"Husband?" she calls. Where is he? She pauses. What is his name? She had known once. He had a name all his own which had been hers to call, hers and hers alone. A secret name. That name was now gone. As was her own. What is happening? All she remembers is that he is her husband and he is the king.

She goes into his study—though what a study is and why he has one is a mystery to her—and finds him sitting at the desk, his face buried in his hands.

"What is happening, abang?" she asks, unable to call him by name. Only able to call him by their relationship.

"It has all gone wrong…" He pauses. He cannot remember her name either then. "What have we done?"

"I don't understand. What has gone wrong? What is happening?"

"We asked her to renew us. We asked her to help us. To bring us into this new modern world of theirs. But the change is happening so fast—too fast—that we are forgetting. We are forgetting who we are."

~

Baba Yaga watches as the scenery before her flickers. The city expands, tall buildings shooting up into the sky. It feels as if a hundred years of development are condensed into three seconds. That can't be right, surely. Around her, the farmlands disappear, the forests shrink. She taps her teeth as she thinks.

Animals run shrieking out of the forest as trees turn into buildings. Some of the animals stop and morph, their eyes aglow in shock and horror. No, something isn't right. What *is* the girl doing?

She sits high up in her house, watching everything around her change. Even the weather is starting to change. A few flakes of snow start and then stop. Snow? Here? The wind howls aimlessly. Baba Yaga selects several herbs from her shelves and puts them into her mortar. Automatically, she starts grinding them as she thinks.

Her house rises on its feet and heads home. Home to where things have remained the same for hundreds of years and change happens with glacial slowness. Something is terribly wrong.

~

For the first time in her life, she feels no hunger. It is a strange feeling. A sort of hollow feeling. She doesn't desire anything more. She stops pacing the stretch of banana trees that she's been haunting for the past sixty-five years. Has it been that long? Why had she been haunting it? The reasons have long slipped her mind. She'd kept on because of her hunger, her driving hunger, and now that has been taken away.

She sits down with a bump, flicking her hair back from her face. She tilts her head upwards and basks in the warm sunlight for a very long time, wondering why she hasn't done this before. Oh yes, because of her hunger. *Why?*

There is a small child standing in the doorway of a nearby hut looking very confused. It starts to cry. The poor thing. It's all alone, without any parents. Where are his parents? Where is her child? Maybe she should look after the poor thing. After all, they are both alone in this strange world.

Everything has changed. But has it changed for the better? She has no driving thirst for blood now, and maybe that is good. But what is there for her to eat and do?

She has no idea. She is adrift.

The baby starts to cry. She picks it up. It wants to nurse, but her dried up body has no milk and no blood. The world doesn't make sense anymore.

~

Euthalia storms angrily down the path. This is ridiculous! Half the trees have disappeared and the other half have forgotten how to speak! She will have words about this. If she can find the culprit. Trees are not just things that decorate a forest. They're not furniture. They are living, breathing beings. They are sentient, even if they do not speak to people.

She pounds on the adlet's door. It swings open and before he can say a word, she starts her tirade.

"Woah, woah, slow down," he says, backing away. "I don't know what you're talking about."

"The world has gone crazy. You should see it for yourself. What has that friend of yours been doing?"

"Who?"

"That girl! The one who was with you from that land."

"Sara?"

"Yes. Whatever her name was. I don't care. You better speak to her right now and make her correct it."

"I don't know how to get to her. And I still don't understand what's the issue."

"She's killed everything, Ataneq. It's becoming some sort of concrete maze in there. Half the trees are dead or dying. And those who aren't can barely speak!"

"And you think she did it? How?"

"I don't know how. It's just happening. And I know it has something to do with her. That's what the trees who can still speak are saying. Get her here right now to fix it!"

"I don't know how, Euthalia! How do I get to her?" His voice is rising in correlation to the level of Euthalia's screams. It really isn't like the dryad. She's normally the calmest being in the world.

Euthalia seems to deflate. "I don't know, Ataneq, but they say Mary's been there. Oh, dear Ataneq, please do something before it's too late."

Ataneq hugs her close. "I'll ask Mary. She must know something."

~

He feels it. A moving. A shaking. A reckoning.

"You must come," she says, but he doesn't know who she is. She is lithe and beautiful, a queen of the trees, an avenger of their shed wood.

"You must come," she says, flickering between long-haired woman and owl. The Lang Suir holds a small body close and he cannot see if it is a Toyol or a real baby.

"You must come," she says, the pounding of her pestle grounding her in reality. Baba Yaga isn't of this land, but she is holding it together for him.

"You must come," he says, and the world grinds to a stop. Abdul Mansoor can tell that he doesn't know who he is talking to, doesn't know who he is asking to come. There is no recognition in those eyes. He is a mindless force, a shadow of his former self.

"I come," he says, and something bucks. Something eases. Something stills.

The world is changing. He will guide its change.

# CHAPTER 20

Abdul Mansoor was pacing when Sara came into the kitchen. She greeted him and poured out a cup of coffee from the ready-made pot.

"Are you going over today?" he asked suddenly, startling her.

"Over?"

"To Alam Dongeng." When she hesitated, he pushed, "You need to, Sara. I don't know what happened last night, but something's changed. I need you to bring me in."

"To… to bring you in?"

He nodded. "There are things I need to fix."

"What do you mean?"

It was his turn to hesitate. He wasn't sure how to explain or even *what* to explain. Before he could think of anything, Helmi came into the kitchen.

Sara turned to him, biting her lip. "Mi, do you think—do you think we could bring your grandfather along?"

"What?" Helmi almost choked on his coffee.

"It's perfect, Mi. He knows the stories. He loves them. He would be able to put things right."

Helmi looked from Sara to Abdul Mansoor. "I suppose it makes sense… but… aren't there rules or something about people going over?"

"Oh yeah," Sara said, her face falling. "Wait—then how are we supposed to go over? What if we get into trouble with the Fairy Queen?"

"We're safe, I think. If I understand Aunty Mary's message right, they're asking us to come over and fix things." He paused. "Well, not exactly come over, but to fix things. I suppose we need to be there to fix it. Because we don't even know what we did."

Sara pulled out her phone and read the message again. "Yeah, I think you're right. Uh, let me ask to see if she knows what we can do to bring your grandfather over."

The answer came almost instantly. "Ask imps to bring him in."

"Imps?" Abdul Mansoor asked.

Helmi too looked confused. "What does she mean?"

Sara frowned at the phone trying to figure it out. Moments later, she looked up, a silly grin on her face. "The—uh—what was it—Kenit? In my house!" She pulled out her wallet where she'd stashed the verse Mary had given her. "The ones Mary said I should make do my bidding!"

"Oh! But we don't even know if that works," Helmi said.

"I guess we'll have to find out."

It took them less than fifteen minutes to wash their mugs, pack some supplies and head out of the house. As Helmi drove, Sara read the verse out loud slowly:

*"The protection of this house is yours, now and forever more.*

*Our sustenance is yours for as long as you need,*

*Our lives are pledged as friend to friend*

*That those who come against you will face our wrath."*

She leaned back in her seat. "What does it mean?"

"It's like a binding oath, Sa. Are you sure you want to do it?" Helmi asked.

"I don't even know if it's applicable here."

"We won't know until we try."

"Why can't we leave things as it is?"

"Why don't I try it? Then it would bind them to me, not to you. And you'd feel safer, yes?"

"It might not work. Remember what Aunty Mary said?"

"Well, she also said she wasn't sure. I think it's worth a try. If it doesn't work then you can have a go. Okay?"

Abdul Mansoor shifted in the passenger seat. "No. It doesn't feel right, this oath. Maybe it works for her, for her land. But it might be dangerous here, to bind them to you and your house in that way."

Helmi didn't reply as he pulled into the guest parking lot, but the frustration was clear on his face. "Then what?"

"I'll talk to them. I've talked to them before."

Sara let out a gasp. "You have?"

Abdul Mansoor nodded. "I'll ask them to show themselves to you."

Once in the apartment, Abdul Mansoor gestured for them to sit. He too took a seat and in a soft voice asked the Kenit to show themselves. Small figures appeared in front of them.

It was the mother who spoke first. "As head of this clan, I apologise for not showing myself earlier, but I wasn't sure if you were able to understand us. I rarely heard you speak in our language, and I did not want to have found a house only to be chased out again."

Sara smiled nervously. "Well, you're welcome here, I suppose, as long as…"

"Our intentions are good," the mother said when Sara didn't continue. "We just want a home. We have long known of the portals in your house and have been trying to keep them close. Unfortunately, the powers of the Orang Bunian and the Hantu far exceed ours, especially when they are working in sync." Mother Kenit's gaze flickered to Abdul Mansoor before fixing itself on Sara again. "The day after you disappeared, we saw a surge of power and went to investigate. We could do nothing against the Bunian royalty, but we kept a look out for you. When you finally reappeared days later, they left you in the walkway in the middle of the night. We brought you home and put you to bed."

Abdul Mansoor kept his face blank, though his thoughts were in turmoil. He heard Sara gasp in surprise.

"I wondered why they would be so nice to put you to bed when they kidnapped you off the streets," Helmi murmured.

"The first night the Toyol came," the Kenit continued, ignoring the interruption, "we distracted him so that he would not harm you. But we could not prevent him from leaving with you. The next night, the apparitions only came to you in your dreams. We held the portal as long as we could, until the Lang Suir came, breaking through the portal and through our charms. Again, we could do nothing against the Raja but hide. We are sorry that we could not do enough."

"But you gave me enough time to call Helmi. You bought me enough time to call for help and that is a great feat," Sara said kindly. Her hand reached over and found Helmi's. "Now, we need your help."

"We will do what is within our means for the protection and shelter you have given us."

"I have made a grave mistake. Words I have written have shaken Alam Dongeng, almost destroying it."

"We felt the shift, but we did not know what it meant."

"Our friends in the Old Fairy Kingdom have called us to the realm to help fix it, but we do not know what to do. We wish to bring Helmi's grandfather with us, for he is a reciter of lore, a greater Penglipur Lara than I could ever be. But the rules of this new fairy kingdom is that each person must be invited. Will you… will you help us bring him in? We do not want to get into trouble or get you into trouble, but we need this favour of you."

Mother Kenit looked at them in surprise. "But he has been invited. He has been called."

Abdul Mansoor frowned. "It was a dream."

"Dream or not, you have been invited."

"The portals—"

"Ah, that we can hold open for you. Come. Let us be on our way."

They headed into the bedroom, where the window still stood wide open, the portal shimmering.

Helmi looked out and down. "This looks very dangerous."

"It's the only way," Abdul Mansoor said. Several of the Orang Kenit went before them. Holding hands, Sara and Helmi stepped through, Abdul Mansoor following closely behind.

# CHAPTER 21

It was an almost-spiritual experience. Abdul Mansoor stepped into Alam Dongeng expecting nothing but receiving everything he had ever dreamed of. From his first breath, the excitement of magic unfolded over him, making his body tingle with anticipation. Everything was as he had left it before, but everything was *different*. New.

"Welcome," they greeted him.

"Wassalam," he replied, bending his head to acknowledge them. "The peace of God be upon you." The trees towered over him, faded as they were, but as he reached out for them, they seemed to become more firm, more real. As he walked, it seemed as if the world became more alive.

When he saw the destruction before him, his heart broke. The city was in ruins, the rainforest entangled in it. Neither the city nor the forest seemed to know what was required of them, what they were supposed to be.

"Be not," he said softly, raising his hand in blessing. The city subsided in front of his eyes, dissolving into nothing but sand. A soft breeze picked it up, scattering it. Mansoor shielded his eyes. In front of him lay nothing but soft, brown earth. He smiled, bent and scooped it up. A thousand small green things grew up, and a fragrance burst forth. Hibiscus.

He picked one and gave it to Sara.

"How did you…" she started saying as her fingers grasped the slender stem.

"This is my world, Sara Liew. This is my dream." He sat down cross-legged on the floor and invited Helmi and Sara to do the same. "Let me tell you a story." He waited for them to sit beside him, the Orang Kenit coming forward to complete the circle.

"Let me tell you all a story!" he announced louder in his story-telling voice. Memories of sitting at his grandfather's feet and listening to stories rushed into Helmi's mind. He reached over for Sara's hand. Various animals appeared from the forest filling in the gaps in the circle: mouse deer, rabbits, mice, tapir, elephants. Even a tiger came, but he sat far away, observing from the distance. The eagles came, as did the hornbill, the crows and the parrots. The crocodile slid into view and a wide space opened for it.

And then Abdul Mansoor began:

"It began a long time ago, when the earth was young and men were few. They were sons of the earth, working the ground for food and gathering from the trees for supplies. They lived near the ground in houses made of wood, not deserts of sand and concrete. It was a time when everyone lived in harmony.

"There was a wise man in those days called Abdul Mansoor. The men of the village would come to him for advice. The women of the village would whisper to his wife to ask him for advice. And the animals would sit at his feet, listening to his wise sayings. Even wise Sang Kancil talked with him as friend to friend. It seemed as if it were a good age, a prosperous time, but Mansoor was worried. He could see far into the future, and that future seemed dim to him.

"It seemed that people were forgetting. They were forgetting who they were, forgetting where they came from. They started building houses of brick; houses with ten rooms for two to stay. They followed the men from the West, the tall, white men that seemed so wise, so beautiful, so cunning. They were like heavenly beings, as glorious as the clouds in the sky. And so they began to hate themselves. They disliked their dark skin, forgetting that they were men of the earth, born of fertile grounds. They discarded their mellifluous tongue, forgetting that they were speaking the language of the birds. And then they left the forests of their youths for the city of their captors, for captives they were, though they did not know it.

"The very people they thought were their saviours, releasing them from the strife of their difficult lives were only enslaving them to new masters. The masters of greed and want. And so the forest grew quiet, for the voices of men were gone. And the creatures who had been their friends and their inspiration soon grew to be nuisances to be killed. A way of life died the day they deserted their past and heritage. And for once, Mansoor's wisdom failed him. He did not know what to do.

"Then he was betrayed. Cast out, his own sons grew up slaves of the new regime, not knowing the glorious past they had left behind, having been too young to have seen it. And now, he was stuck. There was no way back to the past, and there were no more paths in the future. It would seem that all had ended.

"Yet hope has a way of finding one, and Mansoor soon saw that a new path was opening. A new path yet unexplored. He called on his friends of old to help him, but they could hear him no longer, they could understand him no more. This was a path he would have to walk alone. And so he did, telling himself stories of the days past, keeping the memories alive, even if they only lived in one man. He told stories to his children for as long as they would listen, hoping that they would remember something of them, even if it was only a tenth of all he had said.

"But his children and his children's children were blinded. They had gone so far astray that they could not find their way home to him again. Until she came. She was a breath of fresh air, a light in the dark, a beacon that beckoned all to come home, although she did not know what it was she did. All she said was I will try. And it was enough.

"It was enough to change a world. It was enough to sound the alarm. And it was enough to bring me home to you. The world has changed, the world is changing, and the world will yet change. But you, my friends will survive that change."

Abdul Mansoor rose to his feet and he was no longer a simple Malay man living in the past. He rose and spoke with words of power, directing events, directing people and the creatures who sat spellbound at his feet were renewed by his power and his vigour. Now, they dispersed back to their homes with excitement and growing strength.

"Thank you, my children," he said to both Helmi and Sara, embracing them. "Thank you for bringing me home."

"I don't understand, Atuk."

"Do you remember the stories I used to tell?"

Helmi nodded.

"They weren't just stories. They were real-life events in this place. But I was shut out—on forfeit of my life, and after a while, I had no more new stories. Nothing left to share. Nothing but ashes.

"I tried to, but I could not make up any of my own. That is not my power. My power is telling people the truths of what I had seen. And to make that work, I had to see things." He turned to Sara, "Your power, my child, is different. You have the power of making things, and whilst that is very useful and very needful, it is not what Alam Dongeng needs at this point of time. What Alam Dongeng really needs now is an anchor to the past to remember who they are. Once they are assured in that, that is when they will need you—to forge new paths ahead for them. That I cannot do. Thank you for bringing me here. Now, in return, let me introduce this world properly to you."

Abdul Mansoor looked around and picked a path. His stomach curdled. He stilled it. This was something he needed to do. This was a battle he needed to fight, whether he won or… he died. He held tightly to his sense of being, to his strength of beliefs, to his fierce love. The deeper they walked into the Bunian's world, the faster his heart beat, steeling himself for the inevitable. For the axe to drop. As he walked the world righted itself, the destruction it had borne from Sara's clumsy wielding repairing themselves in the face of his strong knowing.

"Will you guide me, Pakcik Mansoor?" Sara asked. "If I am to help, I really need to know everything that you do about this place and the creatures in it."

"Of course, I will, Sara! It would be wonderful to have people listen to me again," he said wistfully.

"None of your grandsons listen to you, eh?" she teased, poking Helmi in the ribs.

"Hey, I listen, okay? Most of the time."

Abdul Mansoor stopped walking abruptly, causing Sara to almost walk into him. She looked up to find that he was staring straight at the Raja and Permaisuri Bunian, a strange look on his face. They too were staring coldly at him, looking as if they had seen a cockroach.

Sara and Helmi bowed in greeting. A second or two later, Abdul Mansoor bowed stiffly, still eyeing them warily. He stamped down his fear, crushed his panic.

"How… interesting to see you here, Mansoor," Raja Bunian said softly.

"You know each other?" Helmi asked incredulously.

"We are acquainted," his grandfather replied in a voice as stiff as his body.

A cruel smile appeared on the Raja's face for a few seconds. He raised his hands and pointed. Wordlessly, an attachment of Bunian soldiers surrounded Abdul Mansoor and Helmi, their swords ready in their hands.

"What's going on?" Helmi demanded.

"When a traitor returns, he must face his crimes," Raja Bunian said with a hiss.

"Let him go," Abdul Mansoor said, his voice a low growl. "He has no fight with you."

He just smirked, gesturing for the soldiers to march them away.

"A traitor? Why is he a traitor?" Sara grabbed at the Raja's arm. "You can't punish Helmi for his grandfather's crimes!"

"Can't we?" The Raja's face was pinched. "They will stand judgement. Tonight." With that, the royal couple turned and disappeared into the forest again, leaving Sara all alone.

"Wait! Come back!" she screamed, chasing after them. They were nowhere to be found.

# INTERLUDE

There is only pain.

# CHAPTER 22

Sara tried to follow the trail the soldiers had left, but that soon disappeared into the underbrush. She was alone in the middle of an unknown magical forest, and she did not know what to do.

She had fallen asleep on that same cursed dais when Garuda flew by. He stopped and perched beside her, nudging her gently with a wing.

"Garuda?" She wiped her bleary eyes. "Oh Garuda, you've got to help us!"

"What's happened now?"

She told him what had happened with Abdul Mansoor and Helmi. A frown spread across Garuda's face.

"Abdul Mansoor? He came back?"

"Yes. You know him? Do you know why they call him a traitor?"

It was a slight pause that told her he knew. All he said was, "Come, let us find Sang Kancil. He knows more than I do."

She followed the bird through the forest into parts she hadn't seen before. Come to think of it, she had barely seen anything of this place, having spent most of her time with the Orang Bunian, or that dreadful time with the Hantu. They found Sang Kancil dozing by the stream.

"What is it, Garuda?" he asked.

"Abdul Mansoor."

"Oh, I heard he was back. Did they catch him? How careless of him."

Garuda gave him a flat stare. "I know he was exiled, but what did he do? Who is he?"

Sang Kancil sighed. "He used to be one of them. A changeling of sorts. And then he fell in love with a human woman and they banished him. I'm surprised that he came back."

"This is my land, he said," Sara said, repeating his words. "He meant that literally. I thought he was just saying that this was his fairy world just as mine was the Western ones!"

"No, I'm afraid that's true. This is his land. You know the Orang Bunian. They kidnapped some poor human child—on purpose or by accident, who knows?—and so he grew up here. He's much older than he looks."

"They said they were going to put him on trial tonight. Where will that take place? Is there any way that we can stop the proceedings?"

Sang Kancil's ears perked up. "An actual trial? They're going to do that?"

"That's what the Raja Bunian said."

"They must believe that they have a strong case." Sang Kancil got to his feet. "Well, we had better prepare then."

"Prepare for what?"

"The trial of course. Mansoor will need a defender. I highly doubt they will provide one for him."

"You're going to take it up? Thank you so much!" Sara flung her arms around the mouse deer, who shied away nervously.

"It's what I do. Besides, they're no match for me. Usually."

Sang Kancil's method of preparation seemed to be walking all over Alam Dongeng asking its inhabitants to talk about Abdul Mansoor. He went first to the crocodiles in the stream, keeping a careful distance from the bank.

"We know nothing of him," they snapped grouchily, upset that they couldn't get at the tender venison that was talking to them.

Next, he talked to the hornbills nesting above them.

"He told us stories," was what they said. "He did us no harm."

The tiger roared at them that Abdul Mansoor always got him into trouble, making him lose dinner too many times.

The rabbits tittered and said he was a good friend. "He helped us escape the tiger so many times! He is such a saviour! Oh, I do hope you get him free," the most vocal of them, a pretty brown bunny said.

"Don't *you* know him, Sang Kancil?" Garuda asked irritably after a while. "Don't you already know why he was exiled?"

"Of course I do. But what we need is witnesses other than me, Garuda. I can't be defence and witness at the same time."

The three continued on until they finally found Sang Kura-Kura.

"Mansoor? Mansoor? Is he the one with the white hair, then? No, the one who talks a lot? Hmmm… he told me a very long story once, I believe," the old tortoise replied. "Very patient old man. Unfortunate that he preferred the other world to this one."

Sang Kancil stopped to consider this. "Tell me more."

The old tortoise settled into a comfortable position, speaking in a slow drawl. "There were two of them at that time. Changelings. One was human, one was Bunian. But they were close friends, growing up together. Brothers, almost. The human had stumbled into our land by accident as a child and the Bunian had taken him in. When the human came of age, he returned to his own world. But things had changed too much for him, and he came back. The Bunian was happy, of course, that his friend had returned. But the time came when the human decided to venture out again. He had a longing for a life and love, for a mate to share with and children to carry on his name. But he could not get that here, of course, not unless a female were to wander in as well for he did not want to kidnap one of his own kind. No, he had principles, not like his friend the Bunian. That was their first argument.

"So Mansoor went back into his world and there, he fell in love. The Raja Bunian of that time grew sick of a strange malady and died in an attack by the Hantu. It is not sure why the Hantu had attacked for there had been peace for a long while, but die he did, and Mansoor's good friend Aria raised himself to be Raja Bunian.

"Mansoor heard of the old Raja's death and returned to pay his last respects. He was greeted kindly by his friend, but their meeting soon grew sour when Mansoor refused to stay. 'I have a family now, a wife and child,' he said. 'I need to return to them.'

"But Raja Bunian refused to let him go. He kept Mansoor locked up in a deep dark cave. Seeking help from his friends in the animal kingdom and hidden friends amongst the Orang Halus, he made his escape. Raja Bunian found out too late to stop him from leaving, but he branded him a traitor and said that if he were ever to come back again, he would be put to death."

The story ended on that ominous note.

"All this because he did not want to stay? But what right does Raja Bunian have to make him stay here against his will?" Sara asked. It was too small an infraction to make sense.

"None," Sang Kancil replied. "If Mansoor is really a human none of us have the right to make him stay. We can ask him to, but it must be his decision. This has been the law since the days of my forefathers. No fairy folk have the right to demand anything of a human. No human has a right to demand anything of our folk. That is how it has always been and how it will always be. There is no other way to keep us from taking advantage of each other."

Garuda nodded in agreement. "We trade in favours. I have done many favours for the kings of old, but they too have done many favours for us. It is the way of our world."

"But why would Raja Bunian do this? I still don't understand. I mean, I would be sad if my friend left and never came back, but I wouldn't try to kill her for it." Sara asked again.

"It is believed that Mansoor knows some secrets about the Raja that he does not want anyone else to find out. He might be trying to kill his friend to protect his throne," Sang Kura-Kura replied.

"Will you be at the trial tonight?" Sang Kancil asked.

The tortoise barely paused before he answered, "Yes, I will leave now."

They thanked Sang Kura-Kura and went on their way. Sara had found out much about Mansoor's past, but she still didn't know the why. Sang Kancil still refused to say anything. It was not until they talked to Sang Gagak that she started to have an idea of what was truly happening.

"In league, you say?" Garuda asked, troubled.

"We have seen them as we flew," the crow answered. "The Raja and his Permaisuri were in deep discussion with Lang Suir, mother of all the Pontianak. It seemed to us like a friendly meeting, not a fight."

Sara frowned, a memory tickling the back of her mind. Someone had said it before. Someone had alluded to such a thing, but she had been preoccupied with something else. Who was it? Who had said it? The vision of her kitchen and the Orang Kenit suddenly flooded her mind.

*"Unfortunately, the powers of the Orang Bunian and the Hantu far exceeds ours, especially when they are working in sync,"* she blurted.

"What?" the three mystical creatures turned towards her in shock.

"That's what they said. That's exactly what they told us."

"Who?" Sang Kancil asked.

"The Orang Kenit. The ones living in my house! We asked them for help. They said that they *had* been trying to help me as the owner of the house, but they were overwhelmed. And then they said that—'when they are working in sync'."

"Are you sure about that?" Garuda asked. "They have never said such a thing to me before."

"I am quite sure," Sara replied emphatically. "It had been an odd thing for them to say but I was distracted with many other things, including how to get Pakcik Mansoor here—but I am quite sure they said that!"

"And so it remains for us to find them and ask them what they know." Sang Kancil turned to Sang Gagak. "Will you testify for us tonight?"

The crow nodded. "For the safety of our land, I will do so." The crow took to the air, calling to its comrades. "To the trial!" they cried as they flew.

Garuda turned to Sara. "Where can we find the Orang Kenit?"

Sara shrugged. "The last I saw them was when we exited the portal and Pakcik Mansoor gathered the crowd to tell his story."

"He is powerful. We cannot let Raja Bunian kill him," Sang Kancil said. "We must return to the clearing to see if they are still there."

They ran, loped and flew as fast as they could, but the Orang Kenit were no longer there. The three of them debated whether they should check back in Sara's apartment, but it didn't seem likely that they would have gone back so fast. Still, it only took a few seconds to pop back and check, so Garuda did that, returning in a minute with a shake of his head.

"They are not there." He thought for a while. "Could they have gone back to their strongholds?"

No one else had any ideas so Garuda led them to the old caves that had once formed the Orang Kenit's home. That too was empty.

Soon Sang Kancil called a stop to the search. "We do not have any other ideas and there is not much time left. We will need to find something to eat before the trial."

Sang Kancil led them back to his stream where they had a quick meal of fruits, drinking of the clean, refreshing water from the stream. Then glumly, they headed to the trial.

# CHAPTER 23

Sara's heart skipped a beat when they came into the circle of firelight. Helmi and Abdul Mansoor were tied back to back against a stake in the middle of the circle. The fire, whilst not directly under their feet, was near enough that the heat from the blaze was searing their skin. It looked as if any strong wind in the wrong direction might end up setting them on fire. She could almost see the sweat bead on their faces. She squinted in the shifting light. Helmi looked tense, worried. His grandfather was bruised and bloodied.

The Orang Bunian had formed a circle around them and seemed to be singing or chanting something. Sang Kancil strode up to them and broke the circle.

"What are you doing here?" Raja Bunian said harshly.

"We are here to see that a fair trial is carried out," Sang Kancil replied calmly, ignoring the flash of anger that spread across the king's fair face.

"Why should my trial not be fair?"

"Because we know you hold a grudge against him. But there is a problem we need to address first. Is not the trial of treason only against Mansoor? What have you against the grandson?"

"Treachery runs in the blood," the Raja hissed. "If the man is guilty, so is his grandson!"

"Treachery is an action, not an illness. By your own words, it has been admitted that this trial is a cheap fakery."

"No!"

"Then let the boy go."

The look on Raja Bunian's face was murderous, but with a short bark and a motion of his hand, his soldiers cut Helmi lose from the stake.

Garuda led him out of the circle to where Sara was. She embraced him, tears in her eyes.

"I'm sorry, Helmi. I'm sorry I got you into all this."

Helmi held her tightly. "It wasn't you. It was all of them. None of this was your fault."

Garuda silenced them with a wave. By now, the crowd around the fire had swelled. Sara could see many of the creatures they had talked to earlier had come to witness the trial. Sang Kancil nodded to Sang Kura-Kura and Sang Gagak who took up places near the front.

"Now, we are gathered here to see a fair trial, are we not?" Sang Kancil addressed the crowd. Various cries of assent arose.

"It seems to me that there should be more than one person on trial then," he continued. "We know that this human Abdul Mansoor has been accused of treason. But there is one more traitor to be put on trial here tonight."

The crowd buzzed with confusion. Sang Kancil waited until he heard more than one cry of "Who? Who's the traitor?" before he turned dramatically and pointed at Raja Bunian.

"You! You who dare call your own friend, your best friend, a traitor. You who said that treachery runs in the blood. You are a traitor to your kingdom and to your own kind."

The Raja surged to his feet, roaring, "You lying rascal!"

"No, it is the truth. I have long suspected that the Orang Bunian were in league with the Hantu, but now I know that it is you."

"You have no proof."

"Do I not? Let me lay the charges and the proof before these good people." He paused. "But first, before that, we should get our friend Mansoor off the hot stand, should we not? Lay out your charges against him that we may decide if he is guilty of treason or not."

It was then that the farce began.

First, the Raja said, "He left the kingdom without my permission."

Sang Kancil sighed. "He is a human, not your subject. He does not need your permission."

"He escaped from prison."

"Which you had wrongly put him there, when he was not your subject."

"He refused to stay when I ordered him to."

"Again, he is not your subject. He does not need to bow to your orders."

"He murdered my father."

"And how pray, did he do that? He was in the human world at that time. Is he a magician that he can send arrows in to Alam Dongeng without being physically here? Oh, pardon me, I'm sorry, your father was murdered by a Pontianak. Are you saying that he is a Pontianak? In secret?"

"He was in collusion with them. They were plotting to kill my father and take over the throne. I stopped them in time and threw him out!"

A grin spread across Sang Kancil's face. "You threw him out. I see. But didn't you just say that he refused to stay when you ordered him to? So, did you throw him out or order him to stay? This is all very confusing."

A look of dread spread over the king's face. "Well, of course I ordered him to stay as my friend, but when I found out his evil plot, then I had to throw him out."

"Hmmmm I see. So, is he on trial now for trying to stay or for trying to leave?"

"He is on trial for being a traitor!" Raja Bunian screamed, losing his patience.

"Yes, but what did he betray?"

"He betrayed me."

Sang Kancil weighed his words for a long moment. Then, with a gentle smile, he said softly, "But you see, my friend, choosing to return home to his wife and child is not a betrayal of you or your friendship. It was a rational choice. You, on the other hand, chose to make it into an issue, pitting him into an "us versus them narrative" which is useless and ultimately destructive. So, I would say that it is you who betrayed him. You who betrayed his friendship and his trust by attempting to use your power and your glamour to make him to your bidding."

"I am not the one on trial here!"

"I would say that you are. Mansoor is innocent. Do you not agree!"

Around him, the crowd cheered in agreement.

"Let him go."

The soldiers reluctantly cut the old man loose. Helmi escorted his shaking grandfather over to where they were sitting. Sara reached out, lightly touching his bruised hands. He winced.

All eyes turned back on Sang Kancil and the Orang Bunian.

"And so we come to our real trial. The trial of the traitor called Aria, now known as Raja Bunian. The traitor who has tried to pin his many sins and many betrayals on everyone else."

"Lies! All lies!"

Sang Kancil ignored him. "This Aria knew that his father favoured the human—his friend, Abdul Mansoor. He was afraid that the old Bunian would try to pass leadership of his kingdom to the human, though that is impossible and illegal. The old Raja was an honourable Bunian. But dishonour does not understand honour, so Aria, in his desperation, started plotting with his wife and with the Hantu to try to take over the kingdom by force. Why would they do this? Let us put it this way. The Permaisuri Bunian, human in original form, has lost child after child after child, some of whom live on in the form of the Toyol. Therefore, she had ties with the Hantu.

"They poisoned him and when he was weak, when his glamour started to fade, their friends came in to finish the job. Abdul Mansoor heard of the death of his mentor—his father figure—so he came back—risked coming back—to pay his last respects. But while he was here, he heard whispers. He grew to be suspicious of his friend. Because how was it that the king—so powerful and strong—could sicken and be killed so easily? He knew it had to be an inside job. A conspiracy.

"Aria heard of his suspicions and became worried. He knew if Abdul Mansoor started digging around and asking questions, he might find out the truth. Therefore, he tried to banish him or to imprison him. Either way would make sure that he did not have access to our Alam anymore. He succeeded and there was peace in Alam Dongeng for a long while. But the Hantu were not satisfied. Aria did not keep his side of the bargain. He was supposed to provide them new haunting grounds, but now that he was king, he found that he could not bear to let go of any of his lands. They started to pressure him. And with the loss of a powerful storyteller, the land began to lose its shape. It began to lose its convictions. It began to lose belief."

"I *saw* it," said Abdul Mansoor, his hoarse voice interrupting Sang Kancil. "She showed me. In a dream."

"Who?" Sang Kancil asked, his gaze spearing Abdul Mansoor's.

"Lang Suir. A few days ago—" Abdul Mansoor shook his head, trying to clear it of the cobwebs. The memory of his dream rose to the surface. "They struck a deal. Aria slipped something into his father's food. Nur opened the door..."

"More lies! You *traitor*," Raja Aria shrieked. "He's admitted it. He's had dealings with the Lang Suir!"

"I did not seek her out. She came to me," Abdul Mansoor said.

"That I did," a new voice answered. Lang Suir stepped out of the shadows. She kept her distance from the fire, standing at the edges of the light. "We had an agreement. It was broken. The world is not as it is supposed to be."

"What was the agreement?" Sang Kancil asked.

Raja Aria hissed. "You would listen to the enemy?"

"It is as you said," the Lang Suir replied. She inclined her head. "Continue. I would like to hear your conclusions."

# CHAPTER 24

Sang Kancil faltered a little as he resumed his speech. "It was not just the loss of Abdul Mansoor. It was also the rapid development of Malaysia and Kuala Lumpur, the colonisation of the country, urbanisation that was taking place—all at the same time—that wiped Alam Dongeng off the collective memory of the country almost in one go, leaving only weak pockets of belief. And Raja Bunian became desperate—so desperate that they tried to coerce a new human into doing their will. Sara."

All eyes turned to Sara. She smiled wanly and waved. Sang Kancil continued.

"Collectively they haunted her, both the Bunian and the Hantu, taking turns to play good cop and bad cop. But what they wanted of her was to remake their world. The Hantu wanted her to give them fertile new grounds to haunt. The Bunian wanted her to change the Hantu, to make them milder, to make them impotent, so that they could continue to rule the world—and rule *them*. But Sara would not do it. Sara could not do it. She was not the right person, she did not have the right knowledge.

"One thing she did right—she managed to connect Alam Dongeng with the wider world of fairy tales. With that, we will have a stronger sense of self, a stronger, wider base for us to live in the world. But we have to expect other changes for there are now other powers who have a stake in all we do.

"Their world is old and well-established. Their magic is strong and powerful. And more than that, they have a strong sense of power and justice."

"Which is why we are here at your farce of a trial," a new voice spoke up. A centaur trotted into view, Mary standing beside him. Sara could see a group of centaurs at the edge of the crowd.

"You have given us a very convincing story, Sang Kancil," the centaur continued. "But do you have proof?"

"Honoured Charon," Sang Kancil addressed him with a little bow. "I have gathered witnesses. They will come and give their evidence. You may cross-examine them."

One by one, Sang Kancil called up everyone they had talked to earlier, and each of them related the things they had seen and heard, building up a convincing case against Raja Bunian. When it was done, the centaurs sat in judgement, discussing what they had heard.

Towards the end, Charon shook his head. "The problem is that most of this is hearsay. Do we not have any witnesses who have seen it directly? Who has dealt with them directly and seen them collude?"

The crowd was silent.

"None? One is all we need to convict him. Otherwise it would be very hard to justify this in a proper Court." The centaurs stood, as if they were about to leave.

"Wait!" a voice called. "I have people here who wish to speak, but they need a translator."

Sara turned to see that it was Abdul Mansoor who spoke, surrounded by the Orang Kenit.

"I would offer myself to translate for you, but then that would be a conflict of interest as I could then be accused of twisting or mis-translating their words."

"That is true," Charon agreed. "For the sake of justice, the humans should not be involved in this. Neither should the Orang Bunian. Is there anyone else who will translate? Sang Kancil?"

The mouse deer nodded. "If you trust me, I will do so for them."

And so the Orang Kenit told their story.

"We had been residents in Sara's house for almost five years when the Orang Bunian approached us. They asked for our help, saying that they had identified our human as someone who would be able to assist them. We heard the details of their request—they needed someone who was good at the English language and could write stories. We did not know if this was true or not because whilst we recognise the language, we were unable to understand or know what it was that Sara truly did. However, we trusted the Raja Bunian, so we said that if this were their need, then we would not oppose it, as long as they did no harm to our human."

A weird feeling settled on Sara upon hearing them call her their human. She didn't know if she should be flattered, or if she should feel insulted, as if she were a pet. Sang Kancil continued translating.

"We started to have our doubts the day they kidnapped her. When Sara did not come home past her usual time, we had gone out to search for her. We saw her getting out of the big metal car and heading up our hill when she was snatched by the Bunian. They did not ask her permission, they did not talk to her. They threw an enchantment over her and whisked her away. That was when we started to worry that they may not have her best interests at heart, no matter what they said.

"They took her for a long time, and when they brought her back, they left her unconscious on the floor. It was up to us to hide her in an enchantment and bring her back to the apartment. Later, Garuda came, but we trusted Garuda from our dealings with him a long time ago, so we did not disturb him. We believe that Garuda has been as deceived by them as all of us have been.

"Although we did not trust the Orang Bunian anymore, we did not suspect that they would have colluded with the enemy. This only became evident later on. There had been a Toyol entry, and we had tried to distract him—a little unsuccessfully—but no harm had come to her. The next day, there was a sustained attack on Sara's house and her person, one that we had no power to stop. The Lang Suir herself opened the portal—we thought it was only the Hantu that had come, but we could not close the portal against her. There was something else holding it open—other magics at work. Magics we knew were distinctively of the Orang Bunian. Then they took her, from right under our noses. As the portal sealed behind them, we saw who it was. The Raja himself. We saw him.

"He has brought harm to our home and broken our trust."

The Orang Kenit faded back into the crowd.

"And so there it is—Raja Aria's betrayal laid bare," Sang Kancil concluded. "Do you need any more proof?"

To everyone's surprise, the Lang Suir moved deeper into the circle of light. Sara had almost forgotten that she was there.

"It is as they say. Aria promised us new lands. He promised us many things. He did not deliver. We believe now that he has always meant to trick us. That he meant us to rise up in war against him so that he can destroy us. We do not want war. We just want to survive." The Lang Suir smiled sadly, turning to Sara. "We apologise for our actions against you. Aria assured us that it was the best way to convince you to come to our aid. We know now that it was wrong. Misguided."

Sara bit at her lower lip, her memories and fear rising up as if to engulf her. Her breath came in sharp, sudden gasps. She clenched her hands, but only realised it when Helmi reached over and tried to ease them open. She nodded once at the woman, lips pinched together.

The Lang Suir nodded back then faced the centaurs, pulling herself up straight. "We submit to your judgement."

The centaurs sat in discussion for a long time.

# CHAPTER 25

"Sara, wake up," Helmi whispered, shaking her gently.

She had fallen asleep, her head on Helmi's lap, as the fairy folk talked long into the night. Now she sat up, yawned and stretched. "What happened?"

"The centaurs decided that Raja Bunian and his wife are guilty. They're going to open up an investigation into the death of his father based on the strength of testimony of Sang Kancil and Sang Kura-Kura who are both respected leaders of the community. Lang Suir has also promised full disclosure of their dealings."

"Oh great! Does that mean that we're free to go?"

Helmi nodded. "They've cleared us of all charges."

"Us?"

"Yes, apparently they had to also discuss and decide if we were colluding with them or if we were merely dragged into a battle not our own."

"That's an interesting way you've put it."

He snorted. "Their words, not mine. It's strange, I tell you, so strange."

"What is?"

"The fact that my grandfather had once lived here for years and years and years. No wonder he has no extended family! I found it strange that whilst everyone's families were so big, all there was left of my grandfather's was himself. It never made sense and all he would say was that they had died."

"I'm sure he's glad to return and reacquaint himself with all his old friends."

"A lot of them have died," Helmi said soberly.

"Died? But aren't they immortal?"

"Not all of them are. And that war with the Hantu which killed the old Raja of the Orang Bunian also killed a lot of his friends. Those that were loyal to the old king. I would have loved to meet them." There was a sadness in his voice that she couldn't place. He sighed. "It's time to go home. It's been a long day and it's nearing morning again. And there's still work."

Sara grimaced. They rose to their feet and headed to where Abdul Mansoor was talking his friends.

"Atuk, we're heading back now. Will you come with us?" Helmi asked.

Abdul Mansoor shook his head. "I'll be staying here for a little while. Help them heal a little. Tell your parents I have things to do. I will come back when I can."

Helmi nodded.

The journey home was uneventful. Sara sighed in relief as they stepped through the portal without anything bad happening or without any strange or horrifying creatures jumping out at them.

"I do hope this means that things will be peaceful from now on," she said.

"I hope so too."

Sara fell asleep again on the ride back to Helmi's house, waking only long enough to stumble up the stairs and into bed. Helmi stood at her bedside watching her chest rise and fall with her long, steady breaths.

His mother came up to him and pulled him away.

"Don't do that. Haven't I told you?"

"Do what?"

"Tempt yourself. It is easy to fall into sin, Helmi. Don't put yourself in harm's way."

Helmi thought about their time in the fairy kingdom and smiled to himself. "Don't worry, mak. We've got this."

"I don't care. My house, my rules. Now where is your grandfather?"


Sara stepped into her apartment. She paused in the doorway, looking around warily. Nothing stirred. Everything seemed to be neatly in place. She closed the door behind her and winced. Everything *shouldn't* be in place. They'd left it in a mess that day when they'd hurried into Alam Dongeng. Nearly a week ago.

But no, the pillows were propped up neatly on the couch, looking as if some interior designer had arranged them for a photo shoot. The kitchen was spick and span, the sink not even holding its usual stray mug. She crossed towards her bedroom, wondering what she'd find.

When she pulled the door open, she gasped. The bed had been fixed and made up, the furniture pulled back into its normal alignment. It was as if nothing had happened. Nothing out of the ordinary, nothing bad. Wiped clean.

"Terima kasih," she murmured. *Thank you.*

She opened her window and looked out at the hills. Normal, real-life hills. Then she turned her face sideways and squinted, her eyes now trained to see *through*, to see into the open portal that led back into Alam Dongeng. With a twist of her wrist, she closed the portal, speaking words of power Abdul Mansoor had taught her to seal it. She'd rather not have anyone stumbling in on her bedroom, thank you very much. The portal in her living room she left alone.

On Friday night, she'd convinced Helmi that she should go home the next day. Dina had invited her to stay on longer, but Sara had declined. After five days, she wanted her privacy, her space, her independence. She put the boxes of food into the fridge—the motherly woman still wanted to fatten her up—and walked over to her desk. While her laptop booted up, she reached over to the small stone that sat beside her mouse pad. Her brows drew together as she stared at it.

Hadn't she thrown it away? Lost it somewhere? Dropped it? She remembered pulling it from her handbag a long time ago. And then it had been out of sight and out of mind. Now it sat neatly on her desk— as what, a reminder? She worried at it until her laptop went to sleep.

Minutes later, she shut it down and went out. There was nothing to write, no story to tell. Abdul Mansoor was rebuilding the world and all she had to do was breathe it in.

# DA CAPO

He hesitates at the edge of the realm. Before him, concrete has filled vast spaces, unrelentlessly claiming every centimetre, shrouded by thick, brown haze. There is the honk of impatient cars in the distance, the rattle of speeding trains, the ceaseless drone of air-conditioning units working desperately to keep their owners cool. Amidst the machinery, he hears the voice of a child.

"Pakcik Mansoor?" Sara calls him softly as he stands in between two worlds.

"Just visiting," he says as he steps into her living room, closing the portal behind him. "I must settle my affairs in this world before I leave again."

She stops short of embracing him, instead lifting his hands to her forehead, a gesture she has seen Helmi perform many times. "You don't plan to return?"

"I have lived a long life, Sara. My children have grown old. My grandchildren have families of their own. I have seen great-grandchildren. There is nothing in this world I still need to do."

She nods slowly.

"There is much I need to accomplish in the Dongeng."

She nods again.

"If you have any need, the door is always open, Sara," he says gently.

She nods, because she can open the door, has opened the door, will open the door.

# ABOUT THE AUTHOR

Anna Tan grew up in Malaysia, the country that is not Singapore. In 2015, she traded in a life of annoying other bean counters for one of annoying the online world with questions about life and death and everything in between. The answer is sometimes 42. Sometimes the answers try to eat you.

When she is not writing or nitpicking over other writers' copy, she can be found reading a book or attempting to organise her room. She can be found online at www.annatsp.com.

# OTHER BOOKS

*Anthologies edited by Anna:*
Love in Penang (Fixi Novo; 2013)
Nutmag: Volume 1 (2016)
Nutmag Volume 2: Coffee or Tea? (2017)
Nutmag Volume 3: Island Living (2018)
Nutmag Volume 4: Transitions (2019)

*Short stories:*
Codes, published in Cyberpunk: Malaysia (Fixi Novo; 2015)
Jentayu's Tear, published in Insignia Vol 4: Asian Fantasy Stories
(BWWP Publishing; 2017)
The Longest Mile, published in With Our Eyes Open (Bausse Books;
2017)
When Winds Blow Cold (2015)
The Flame of the North (2017)
Beneath the Rumbling Earth (2017)
A Still Small Voice (2018)
Takpe, published in A Kind of Death (Uncommon Universes Press;
2019)

*Novellas:*
Coexist (2016)

Jane Hays has been told all her life that it's dangerous to be out in the forest past sundown. At fifteen, she's quite sure that it's all old wives' tales... yet, why does her village bar the gates every night? Why do they even *have* gates? When she is caught in an unexpected rainstorm on her way home, Jane ignores all the warnings and seeks shelter in a cottage in the middle of the forest. Soon, she is caught up in a world of magic and beauty—and in the storm of the Fairy Queen's wrath.

The Fairy Queen is out for blood. There have been intruders—*human* intruders—in her domain and she will stop at nothing to find them and kill them. After all, it is only fair. She is only seeking retribution for the death that humans leave in their wake.

But Jane isn't all that she seems to be. And the events of the night aren't as innocent as they appear.

A tale of magic, fairy creatures and family, **Coexist** is a novella for the young and the young-at-heart.

For updates on upcoming books, subscribe to Anna's mailing list:
http://www.annatsp.com/mailing-list.html

You'll also receive a free ebook copy of *When Winds Blow Cold*.

*Go north, little human.*
*Go north until the winds blow cold and you walk on water.*
*Go north, and there you will find her.*

With the Dragon's prophecy ringing in his ears, Danis travels from town to town, seeking a wife. But at every stop, he is turned away, until he enters the City of Winter itself...

*When Winds Blow Cold* is an old-school fairy tale designed to open your eyes to wonder.